VIRGIN BRIDES

WAITING FOR THE WEDDING

Carla Cassidy

Silhouette
ROMANCE™
Published by Silhouette Books
America's Publisher of Contemporary Romance

To Kathryn,
who lights up my life as
only a two-year-old can...
with giggles and tantrums,
and sweet little kisses.
I love you!

 SILHOUETTE BOOKS

ISBN 0-373-19426-9

WAITING FOR THE WEDDING

Copyright © 2000 by Carla Bracale

Visit us at www.romance.net

Printed in U.S.A.

Kay

Sherry's mind filled with memories of how it had once been between them...

the sweet, explosive passion they'd enjoyed, the difficulty in halting because of Sherry's desire to be a virgin on their wedding night.

She wished now she hadn't been so adamant about wanting to be a virgin bride. She wished she'd allowed their passion to sweep them beyond reason. How she wished just once, she'd allowed control to slip, allowed their heated caresses to blossom into complete lovemaking.

But perhaps it was best this way, that she didn't have the memory of making love with Clint to further torment her....

Dear Reader,

Not only is February the month for lovers, it is the second month for readers to enjoy exciting celebratory titles across all Silhouette series. Throughout 2000, Silhouette Books will be commemorating twenty years of publishing the best in contemporary category romance fiction. This month's Silhouette Romance lineup continues our winning tradition.

Carla Cassidy offers an emotional VIRGIN BRIDES title, in which a baby on the doorstep sparks a second chance for a couple who'd once been *Waiting for the Wedding*—their own!—and might be again.... Susan Meier's charming miniseries BREWSTER BABY BOOM continues with *Bringing Up Babies*, as black sheep brother Chas Brewster finds himself falling for the young nanny hired to tend his triplet half siblings.

A beautiful horse trainer's quest for her roots leads her to two men in Moyra Tarling's *The Family Diamond*. *Simon Says... Marry Me!* is the premiere of Myrna Mackenzie's THE WEDDING AUCTION. Don't miss a single story in this engaging three-book miniseries. A pregnant bride-for-hire dreams of making *The Double Heart Ranch* a real home, but first she must convince her husband in this heart-tugger by Leanna Wilson. And *If the Ring Fits...* some lucky woman gets to marry a prince! In this sparkling debut Romance from Melissa McClone, an accident-prone American heiress finds herself a royal bride-to-be!

In coming months, look for Diana Palmer, a Joan Hohl-Kasey Michaels duet and much more. It's an exciting year for Silhouette Books, and we invite you to join the celebration!

Happy Reading!

Mary-Theresa Hussey

Mary-Theresa Hussey
Senior Editor

Please address questions and book requests to:
Silhouette Reader Service
U.S.: 3010 Walden Ave., P.O. Box 1325, Buffalo, NY 14269
Canadian: P.O. Box 609, Fort Erie, Ont. L2A 5X3

CARLA CASSIDY

is an award-winning author who has written over thirty-five books for Silhouette. In 1995, she won Best Silhouette Romance from *Romantic Times Magazine* for *Anything for Danny*. In 1998, she also won a Career Achievement Award for Best Innovative Series from *Romantic Times Magazine*.

Carla believes the only thing better than curling up with a good book to read is sitting down at the computer with a good story to write. She's looking forward to writing many more books and bringing hours of pleasure to readers.

Dear Reader,

I was thrilled when I discovered my book *Waiting for the Wedding* was going to be part of the VIRGIN BRIDES series.

To me, there is something intensely romantic about a heroine who experiences for the first time the wonder of lovemaking with the hero—the man who will be her first, her last, her only.

Sherry Boyd is a special heroine, a woman who has given up her dreams of a wedding, a family and a future with small-town sheriff and ex-boyfriend Clint Graham. How wonderful it was for me to get to play matchmaker and see that these two loving people got their happily-ever-after.

I hope you enjoy their story and that you will find your own special happily-ever-after!

Best wishes,

Carla Cassidy

Chapter One

The last thing Sheriff Clint Graham expected to see when he opened his front door on an early April morning was a baby on his doorstep. Yet, there she was, a bundle of sleeping baby wrapped in a pink blanket and resting in a car seat. Next to the car seat on the wooden porch was a small diaper bag.

Clint looked around. The sun was just peeking over the horizon, promising another glorious spring day. The light of a new dawn painted the tidy homes on his street in a lush, golden light. It was the kind of day that reminded him why he loved the small town of Armordale, Kansas.

He eyed the house on the left, then the house on the right. He knew his neighbors on both sides, knew they probably weren't responsible for the surprise package. He studied the shrubs and trees, seeking the person who'd left the baby.

Nobody. There was nobody around, no cars parked on the street, no strangers lurking in the shadows. Nothing seemed amiss. Except there was a baby on his porch.

Unsure exactly what to do, Clint carefully picked up the car seat and carried the baby into the kitchen. He set the seat on the kitchen table and stared at the cherubic little face.

Pale wisps of blond hair adorned the top of her head. Her cheeks were rounded, her lips little rose-buds that trembled slightly with each breath. He had no idea who she was, how old she was or why she'd been left on his porch.

It was then he noticed the white edge of a folded piece of paper tucked into her blanket. Gingerly he pulled it free, not wanting to awaken her.

He opened the note, frowning as he read.

I've never asked you for anything since Kathryn was born. I've never asked you to be a husband to me or a father to her, but now I need your help. I'm in danger and must be gone for a week or two. Please keep her safe for me. When things are back to normal, I'll return for her, then she and I will once again disappear from your life.

His heart thudded to a halt. The note wasn't signed.

Was it possible? For a brief moment crazy thoughts filled his head.

No, surely not. He'd have heard something. Somebody would have told him. Somehow he'd have known. He shoved aside his momentary, outrageous thoughts.

He stared at the letter again. It was written on plain white notebook paper. There was no clue as to who might have written it. He set it aside, his frown deepening.

Danger. The note said there was danger. Had the mother dropped the baby off here because Clint was sheriff? Before he had time to fully assess the situation, there was a knock on his door.

He hurried to answer, afraid the discordant noise would awaken the slumbering infant. He opened the door and held a finger to his lips.

"What's the matter?" Andy Lipkin, Clint's deputy whispered. He held two foam cups in his hands, steam rising from the hot coffee.

It had become routine for the two men to ride together to the sheriff's station. Andy bought the coffee in the mornings, and Clint bought the sodas on the drive home in the evenings.

"Follow me and be quiet." Clint motioned Andy into the kitchen. Andy stopped short in the doorway as he spied the baby in the center of the kitchen table. On tiptoe, the big, burly man walked toward the table. "What's that?" He set down the two coffees.

"Looks like a baby to me," Clint replied dryly. "She was left on my doorstep a little while ago." He handed Andy the note that had accompanied the surprise bundle.

Andy scanned the note, then handed it back to Clint. "You know who she is?"

"I don't have a clue," Clint exclaimed.

"So, what are you going to do?"

"I don't know," Clint replied. He stared thoughtfully at the sleeping little girl, then looked back at his deputy. He didn't even want to think of what would happen when she awakened. He sighed and raked a hand through his hair. "You go on into the office, and I'll figure something out here. I'll try to come in by noon."

Andy grabbed one of the coffees, and together he and Clint tiptoed out of the kitchen. "You going to call Social Services in Kansas City?" Andy asked.

Clint frowned, thinking of that sweet little baby being swallowed by the system. It was possible if he turned Kathryn in to Social Services, Kathryn's mother would never get the little girl back. Until he knew the mother's identity and the circumstances of the temporary abandonment, he hated to do anything so final.

"Not immediately," he said thoughtfully. "I'd like to try to figure out what's going on before I go the Social Services route. This is a small town, and usually people know each other's business. Maybe somebody will know what's going on with this baby and her mother.''

Andy nodded. "Okay, I'll get out of here." He walked to the door and opened it, then looked back at Clint. "So, if anybody calls and needs you, I should just tell them you're playing nanny for the day?" He grinned.

"You tell anyone that, and I'll file the points off your badge. Now, get out of here," Clint said with a laugh. "I'll call you later."

After Andy had left, Clint went back into the kitchen and once again stared at the baby.

Who was she? Kathryn who? Where was her mother? What kind of danger threatened her enough to leave her baby on a doorstep?

He couldn't very well play nanny for the next week or two. If he didn't intend to turn little Kathryn over to Social Services, then he'd need to make other arrangements.

Sherry. The name instantly came to mind, bringing with it an enormous sense of relief. She would help. After all, she was his best friend.

Without giving himself a chance to think twice, he picked up the receiver and dialed her number.

She answered on the third ring, her voice deeper, husky from sleep.

"Did I wake you?" he asked.

"No. The phone did," she said dryly. "What time is it?" He heard the rustle of sheets, then a squeal of outrage. "Clint Graham, how dare you call me at seven o'clock in the morning. You know I don't do mornings.''

"And you know I wouldn't have called if it wasn't important," he replied.

Again he heard the rustle of bedclothes, and, unbidden, his mind filled with a vision of her in bed. Her streaked blond hair would be tousled and flowing down her shoulders. Her cheeks would be sweetly flushed. Her vivid green eyes would be drowsy with half sleep—sexy bedroom eyes.

"Clint?" Her voice held an edge of aggravation, letting him know she'd probably called his name more than once.

He shook his head, dislodging the crazy image. Where had that come from? It had been a long time since Sherry'd had long hair, and he'd never actually seen her in bed. He'd stopped those kinds of fantasies long ago.

"I'm here," he said.

"I asked you what's so important it couldn't wait until a reasonable hour?"

"Darlin', for most people seven o'clock in the morning is a reasonable hour."

"If you don't tell me in the next ten seconds why you called, I'm going to hang up and go back to sleep."

Clint could tell by her tone of voice that she wasn't kidding. "I have a sort of situation here, and I need your help. Can you come over?"

"Clint? Are you all right?" Her irritation was

gone, replaced by worry. "You haven't caught that nasty flu again, have you?"

"I'm fine. Nothing is wrong, I'm not sick and I really hate to get into it over the phone. Come over, Sherry. You haven't even seen my new place. I'll make you a big breakfast—biscuits and gravy," he said.

"I smell a rat in the house," Sherry exclaimed. "The last time you cooked me biscuits and gravy you asked me to take care of a 'little' of your laundry."

Clint laughed. "I was sick," he protested. "I didn't realize so much laundry had piled up. I promise this involves no heavy work."

"Okay…give me half an hour and I'll be there," she agreed, then hung up.

Clint also hung up, and gave a sigh of relief. Sherry could help him decide what to do. He leaned back in his chair, his thoughts filled with the woman he'd just spoken to.

It was odd. Five years ago he'd believed she was the woman he would spend the rest of his life with, that they would marry and have a family and live happily ever after. It was odd that when their plans hadn't worked out, they'd managed to put love behind and hang on to friendship.

There was very little left of the Sherry he'd fallen in love with years before. She'd undergone a dramatic transformation, one that had begun the day she discovered she would never have children of her own.

Clint frowned and stared at the baby. Maybe calling Sherry hadn't been such a great idea. As if in agreement, little Kathryn's eyes opened wide. She took one long look at him. Her lower lip trembled, her face turned red. She opened up her mouth and wailed.

Sherry Boyd took a fast shower, dressed, then jumped into her car and headed toward Clint's new place. Two weeks before, he'd moved from an apartment into a nice three-bedroom ranch house on Main.

As she drove, she tried to think of what situation Clint had that would demand her presence, but nothing concrete came to mind.

Turning left on Main, she stifled a yawn with the back of her hand. She'd worked until three that morning, and her body felt the effects of too little sleep. Her eyes felt grainy, her feet ached from the long hours of waitressing, and a light headache pounded at her temples.

"This better be good, Sheriff Graham," she said aloud as she spied his house in the middle of the block ahead.

She and Graham had lived in the same apartment building for the past four years, up until two weeks ago when this gem of a house had come up for sale.

Within days Clint had bought the house and arranged his move.

It was a pleasant, white ranch with black shutters adorning the windows. Spring flowers were already pushing up, adding a splash of color against the white siding.

Sherry heard a baby wailing the moment she opened her car door and stepped out. Instantly she tensed and felt a wind blow through her, the desolate wind of barrenness, a mournful cry of what would never be.

The noise couldn't be coming from Clint's place, she reasoned. It was just a trick of the wind. Probably one of the neighbors had a small child.

She reached the front door and knocked, the baby cry louder than before. "Clint?" she yelled. When there was no immediate response, she opened the door and stepped inside.

Clint appeared in the kitchen doorway at the same instant, a sobbing baby girl in his arms. "Thank God you're here," he exclaimed.

For a few seconds Sherry merely stared at him, her mind working to make sense of the scene. Clint's dark hair stood on end, and the front of his shirt was wet with what she suspected was either baby spit-up or slobber.

It was difficult to see exactly what the baby looked like. Her face was bright red at the moment, her features all scrunched up with her unhappiness.

"What's going on?" Sherry asked. She remained

standing where she was, refusing to hold her arms out for the baby, even though she knew that was probably what Clint wanted.

For the past five years, Sherry had made conscious choices that would keep her from being in the presence of children. She'd quit her third-grade teaching job and now worked as a waitress in the town's most popular tavern. She chose her friends carefully, usually people with either no children, or older kids.

"I can't make her stop crying," Clint said frantically. As he talked, he jiggled the baby in his arms. Up and down, up and down, the motion made Sherry feel half-sick, and she had a feeling it wasn't soothing the baby at all.

"Is she wet?" Sherry asked, still not moving a single step forward.

"I don't know. I'm wet. She must be," Clint replied, raising his voice to be heard above the sobbing child.

Sherry could stand it no longer. Despite her reluctance, she moved to where Clint stood, and took the baby from him. The little girl snuggled against Sherry's chest, her sobs ebbing as if she was comforted by the feminine arms.

As the baby quieted, Sherry fought her impulse to scream at Clint, to vent the anger, the sense of betrayal that swirled inside her. How dare he! How dare he call her over here to help him with a baby.

He knew more than anyone the utter torment

she'd gone through when she'd discovered she would never get pregnant, never carry a baby inside her, never have a child of her own. How dare he bring her here where a baby was present, knowing her own particular heartache.

"Come on in the kitchen," he said. "I think there are diapers and stuff in there."

"Are you going to tell me what's going on? Who is she?" Sherry asked as she followed him into the cheerful kitchen, where the morning sunshine streamed through the windows.

"Her name is Kathryn, and that's about all I know," Clint replied. "If you'll take care of her for a few minutes, I'll start the biscuits and gravy."

Sherry sat at the table and waved one hand, dismissing the idea. "I'm not hungry. What do you mean, that's about all you know?"

Clint leaned against the sink cabinet and plucked at his wet shirtfront. "She was on my doorstep this morning." He pointed to the diaper bag. "There should be stuff she needs in there."

Sherry didn't move. "What do you mean, you found her on your doorstep?" She felt ridiculous, echoing him in an effort to get answers.

She looked down at the baby and found herself staring into the biggest, bluest, most trusting eyes she'd ever seen. Sherry flinched, her heart lurched, and she stiffened in defense.

She didn't want to be here. She didn't want to hold this sweet little bundle in her arms. It only served to remind her of her loss and aching emptiness and dreams shattered.

Clint raked a hand through his hair, again making the dark, rich strands stand on end. "When I opened the door this morning, there she was. She was in a car seat, and a diaper bag was next to her. There was a note tucked inside the blanket." He gestured to a piece of paper on the table.

Sherry shifted the wiggling baby in her arms and picked up the note. She scanned the contents, the words creating a strange, new ache in her. She placed the note back on the table, then looked at Clint.

"Is she yours?" she asked softly. The question hung in the air between them.

Clint's face blanched and he swiped a hand across his lower jaw. "I don't know," he finally said. "I've consciously not thought about the possibility since the moment I read that note."

"You'd better think about it now," Sherry replied, fighting the odd ache the note had evoked. She'd wanted Clint to have children of his own, that's why she'd broken their engagement so long ago.

"It's hard to know, since I don't know how old Kathryn is," he replied.

Sherry shifted the baby from one arm to the other. As she did, she felt the warmth of a soggy diaper. She stood and placed Kathryn on her back on the table, then reached into the little bag and withdrew a diaper.

"I'd say she's about six months old," Sherry observed as she wrestled to change Kathryn, who laughed and kicked her feet. "So, who were you dating about fifteen months ago?" she asked.

Clint walked from the sink to the window. For a long moment he stared outside, his broad shoulders blocking the warm stream of sunshine. When he turned back to look at her, his brow was creased in thought. "It had to have been Candy."

Sherry grimaced. Candy. The sexy divorcee from Kansas City. Sherry had hated the attractive, flirtatious woman the moment she'd met her. "Well, the note says the mother is in danger, that's certainly not out of the question where Candy is concerned. She's probably being threatened by some poor wife whose husband Candy was sleeping with."

The left corner of Clint's mouth rose upward. "You never did like Candy," he observed.

"That's probably the understatement of the year," she returned. She finished with the diaper, then set Kathryn on her belly on the floor next to the table. "She was a man-eater, and you were her main dish." Sherry closed her mouth, not wanting to say anything more, aware that the woman she was talking about just might be the mother of Clint's child.

"Right now this is all speculation," Clint said,

his gaze on Kathryn, who was on her hands and knees and rocking as if by will alone she could scoot across the floor. He looked up at Sherry. "It's possible the mother chose to leave her here because I'm sheriff, not because I'm related in any way."

"Yeah, and it's possible tomorrow I'll be voted mayor of this town," Sherry replied dryly.

She stood, needing to escape from this conversation, from the little girl who sat looking up at her as if somehow Sherry was her salvation. "She's stopped crying now, her diaper is clean. Looks like you're on your own, Sheriff Daddy." She started for the kitchen door.

"Sherry...wait!" His voice held a note of utter panic. "I've got a favor to ask you."

"No. Whatever you're about to ask, the answer is no. You can cook me biscuits and gravy every morning for the rest of my life and the answer is going to be no." She left the kitchen and headed for the front door.

"Sherry, please wait a minute. Hear me out," he called after her.

She didn't stop. She left the house and walked hurriedly toward her car. She had a feeling she knew exactly what he wanted, and there was no way, no how.

She'd just slid behind the steering wheel when Clint came barreling out of the house, Kathryn crying in his arms.

He raced to her open window. "Sherry, I need

your help," he said, once again having to raise his voice to be heard about Kathryn's cries. "I need somebody to help me with her until I can figure out what's going on. I need you to take off work a couple of days, stay here and help me out."

"You're crazy," she exclaimed, trying to ignore the plea in his gorgeous blue eyes. "What do I know about taking care of a baby?" she asked, trying to keep the bitterness from her voice.

"You knew which end to diaper," he returned evenly. "I imagine you can figure out which end to feed. What else do you need to know?"

Sherry said nothing.

"I'll pay you for your time…whatever your average earnings at the bar are, I'll double them. Sherry, I'm desperate here. I can't stay home for the next several days and leave this town without a sheriff."

Sherry wanted to tell him it was his problem, that it was really none of her concern. She wanted to slam the car into reverse and escape, but she didn't. She sighed wearily and rubbed the center of her forehead—a headache was just beginning to send tentacles of pressure around her head.

"Sherry." Clint leaned down, so close she could see the silvery flecks that made his eyes so startlingly blue, close enough that she could smell the familiar scent of his pleasant cologne.

"Sherry, please. If you care about me at all, do this for me." He lightly stroked the top of the baby's head. "If...if she is mine, you're the only one I'd trust to watch her."

Something in his eyes, something in their soft appeal, touched her in places in her heart she thought no longer existed.

In an instant of staring into his eyes' blue depths, she remembered too many moments from the distant past, too many dreams that would never come true.

Damn him. She knew exactly what he was attempting to do. He was calling not only on their friendship, but on the love they'd once felt for each other.

And in that instant she thought she might hate him just a little bit, for knowing her well enough to be able to try to manipulate her emotions.

He reached out and curled his fingers around her wrist. His fingers were warm against her skin—skin that she knew was frigid and achingly cold.

"Please, Sherry," he entreated. "You'll never know how much it will mean to me," he said. "I've never really asked you for anything before now."

She jerked her arm away from him, her anger returning to sustain her original decision. "And you, of all people, should realize just what you're asking of me," she returned, trying to keep her tone cool and even. "You, of all people, should know I can't do this. I'm sorry."

Without waiting for any reply, she shifted the car into reverse and pulled out of the driveway.

Chapter Two

Clint stared after the disappearing car, Kathryn's cries a resounding siren in his ears. He looked at the baby in his arms. Once again her face was red, her eyes squeezed shut as high-pitched noise spewed from her little mouth. How could something so small make such an incredible amount of noise?

Her cries momentarily overrode Clint's feeling of guilt. He carried the baby back into the house, trying to avoid thinking about the look on Sherry's face as she'd driven off.

A bottle. Maybe the baby was hungry. He mentally corrected himself. Kathryn…her name was Kathryn. He placed her back in her car seat, buckled her in, then rummaged through the diaper bag. "Ah-ha!" he proclaimed in triumph as he pulled out an empty plastic bottle. Milk. Didn't all babies drink milk?

He poured milk into the bottle, then frowned. Warm or cold? Damn. He was clueless when it came to these kinds of things.

He placed the bottle in the microwave for a few seconds to take off the chill, then sat down at the table and offered the bottle to Kathryn.

Magically her crying stopped. Her big blue eyes widened and her fingers opened and closed as if urging him to place the bottle where it counted.

Clint did just that, and sighed in relief as she gulped the liquid hungrily. Now that her cries had stopped, Clint was faced with his remorse over Sherry.

It had been thoughtless of him to call her, foolish not to think about how painful this all might be to her. Hell, he'd thought she'd come to terms a long time ago about not being able to have children.

He sighed, remembering her pale face as she'd driven away. Her pain-filled eyes haunted him. But he hadn't known what else to do. He hadn't dated anyone for a month, had no family members he could call upon for help.

It had been sheer instinct to contact Sherry for help. He'd called her when he'd had the flu. She'd been there for him when his best friend had died. For the past five years Sherry had helped him through each life crisis that had come his way. It had only been natural that he'd called her for this particular crisis.

She would be back. Despite his guilt, despite her parting words to him as she'd driven away, he knew she'd return. She wouldn't let him down. She never had.

"Is she yours?"

The question Sherry had asked him returned to haunt him. He'd consciously not thought about the possibility from the moment he'd seen the baby on his porch. Now he could think of little else.

He stared at the little girl, whose eyes stared back solemnly. Was she his child? Had Candy had a baby, his baby, and never even told him?

He couldn't imagine a woman doing such a thing—having a baby and not informing the father. But Candy had been nothing if not unpredictable. Besides, who understood the forces that drove women to do what they did?

He touched one finger to a chubby little cheek, his heart constricting with an alien emotion. "Are you mine?" he asked softly. The only reply was soft sucking sounds and a single blink of those wide, blue eyes.

She drank almost the entire bottle, then her eyes drifted closed and she fell back asleep. For a few minutes Clint simply stared at her, trying to see if the mark of his fatherhood showed anywhere on her features.

She had blue eyes, like his own. But his hair was

dark and Kathryn's was a pale strawberry blond. Of course, Clint had been told that he'd been born with a headful of blond ringlets.

He sighed. It was impossible to tell if she looked like him. At the moment she simply looked like a content baby.

Knowing that she was sleeping soundly, Clint got up from the table and went into the spare bedroom. He'd done nothing with this room since moving in two weeks before. The bed was bare, the dresser and old rocker dusty.

Knowing in his heart Sherry wouldn't let him down, he quickly made up the bed with fresh sheets, then dusted the few pieces of furniture the room contained.

He'd just finished with the room when he heard a knock on the front door. Sherry stood on the front porch, a small suitcase in hand.

"Three days," she said as she stepped inside. Her delicate features were pulled taut in a combination of rebellion and determination. "That's all I'm giving you. Three days, then you'll have to figure something else out."

"Sherry—"

She held up a hand. "Don't thank me. I'm not happy about this, but I can't stand the thought of that baby being turned over to Social Services, or worse, baby-sat by you and that dingbat deputy of yours."

He nodded, knowing better than to say anything.

He was just grateful she'd come. "I'll show you to
the spare bedroom," he said, gesturing her to follow him down the hallway.

He opened the door to the room, and she stepped
in. She sniffed, then turned and eyed him accus-
ingly. "I smell lemon wax. You just dusted. You
knew I'd be back."

He smiled sheepishly. "I hoped." He could tell
it annoyed her. Her jaw tightened, and her green
eyes blazed a warning.

She set her suitcase on the bed. "Three days,
Clint. I swear that's it. You find that man-eater
Candy and figure out what's going on."

"No problem," he agreed instantly. Together
they walked back into the kitchen. Sherry barely
looked at the sleeping child.

"I fed her a bottle of milk. It seemed to satisfy
her," he explained. He grabbed his keys from the
holder next to the refrigerator. "I've got to get to
work. Andy's holding down the fort, and who
knows what he'll mess up."

He waited for one of her smiles in return, but
none was forthcoming. He sighed, wondering how
long she would punish him. "I'll be home for supper by six."

Minutes later as Clint drove to the Armordale
Sheriff's Office, his mind whirled with thoughts of
Sherry and the baby.

If he were honest with himself, he'd admit that
he'd never understood the depth of Sherry's pain

when she'd discovered that a severe case of endometriosis had left her unable to have children. In any case, that had been five years before. He'd thought she'd come to terms with that pain, but the look in her eyes when she'd seen baby Kathryn told him otherwise.

Clint had never thought much about having kids. Years before, when he and Sherry were making lifetime plans together, he'd talked theoretically about having children, but it had never been a driving, burning need inside him.

When Sherry had called off their wedding plans, he'd tried to convince her that he didn't care whether or not she could have children, that he would be satisfied just having her in his life. But that hadn't been enough for her. She had insisted that her feelings for him had changed, that she no longer loved him. He hadn't been enough for her.

He shoved these thoughts away. They came from a distant past, one he rarely thought of anymore. He and Sherry had managed to put aside their romantic feelings for each other and build a caring, special friendship.

He parked before the small, brick building that was his home away from home. As he got out of the car, he only hoped he hadn't in some way jeopardized that special friendship by asking her this latest favor.

Sherry stood at the kitchen window, her back to the sleeping infant, wondering why in the heck she had agreed to this.

When she'd pulled out of Clint's driveway earlier, she'd been adamant that she wouldn't return,
that he was asking far too much of her.

She'd gone back to her apartment and had desperately tried to ignore thoughts of the little girl,
those sweet chubby cheeks, those trusting blue
eyes, the natural way the infant had snuggled into
Sherry the moment she'd taken the baby in her
arms.

Before she knew what she was doing, Sherry had
packed a bag and called her boss at the bar to re-
quest the next week off. Madness. Sheer madness.

She turned away from the window and stared at
the sleeping child. Wispy blond hair adorned the
top of her head, and her tiny lips were curved into
a smile, as if her dreams were pleasant.

Sherry would change her diapers, feed her when
she was hungry, but she refused to allow her heart
to get involved. It was the only way she would be
able to get through the next couple of days. She
had to keep a high, impenetrable barrier around her
heart.

She frowned, remembering his parting remark—
that he'd be home for supper around six. What did
he think? That he'd suddenly acquired a wife for
the next three days? If he thought she was going to
cook and clean for him as well as look after the
baby, he had another think coming!

The day passed quickly. The baby slept until almost noon, then Sherry fed her another bottle, set her on the floor of the living room on a blanket and gave her some plastic spoons, lids and small bowls to play with. However, the baby eschewed the makeshift toys in favor of playing with her toes.

Sherry knew what she was doing...thinking of the baby as "the baby" instead of as Kathryn. She was keeping her distance, refusing to allow her heart to get caught up in the wonder of a child.

Kathryn was a good baby. She occupied herself, playing first with her toes, then attempting to catch the afternoon sunbeams that shone through the window.

When she fell asleep once again, Sherry covered her with a light blanket, then stroked the fine, downy hair atop her head.

Was she Clint's baby? Sherry's heart jumped a bit at the thought. There had been a time when she'd dreamed of carrying Clint's child, a time when the possibility had filled her with joy and awe.

Clint had said it was possible Kathryn was his. That meant Clint and Candy had slept together.

Sherry frowned, wondering why that should bother her. She'd long ago quit fantasizing about making love with Clint. She'd long ago quit fantasizing about making love to anyone.

She figured she was probably the oldest living virgin in Armordale. Twenty-eight years old and she'd never been lost in mindless passion. Twenty-eight years old and she'd never experienced the total possession of a man's lovemaking.

It wasn't that she hadn't had offers to rectify that particular condition. Every night at least one half-drunk cowboy professed his undying love for her and offered to take her home and show her delights beyond her imagination. Unfortunately, she had too good an imagination.

She figured maybe someday she'd meet an older, divorced man, one who'd already had his family and wanted no more children. In the meantime she wasn't holding her breath.

By five o'clock Kathryn was fussy and Sherry assumed it was probably hunger. With the baby once again safely buckled into the car seat, Sherry stared at the contents of Clint's refrigerator.

It definitely showed the eating habits of a bachelor. Milk...mustard...ketchup and a pound of hamburger thawing in plastic wrap. She knew Clint ate most of his meals down at the Armordale Café, but he'd obviously planned on something with the hamburger for dinner.

Fine. He and the hamburger were on their own. In the cabinet she found a can of tuna, canned peas and peaches. She made herself a tuna sandwich, then mushed up peas and cut the peaches into tiny pieces for Kathryn. She made a mental note to tell Clint to pick up some baby cereal and food.

As she fed Kathryn, the little girl opened her

mouth like a baby bird awaiting a worm. She tried to help Sherry, grabbing for the spoon, laughing when she managed to grasp it.

"Don't be so cute," Sherry said, finding the little girl's laughter infectious, her antics far too adorable to ignore. Kathryn kicked her feet and grinned, displaying the tiny white nub of a first tooth.

Sherry was grateful when dinner was over. She wiped Kathryn's face, cleaned the kitchen, then deposited the baby back on the blanket in the center of the living room floor.

"I'm only here for a couple of days," she said to Kathryn, who sat facing her, a wide grin still curving her rosebud lips.

Sherry turned her head away from the smiling little girl. "I don't want to care about you," she whispered to herself, as if afraid the child might hear, might understand and be hurt.

Kathryn laughed, as if to get Sherry's attention. Sherry felt a sudden sting of tears. "If I let you, you'll break my heart. I can't let that happen." Kathryn laughed again, as if Sherry had just said something extraordinarily witty.

The distant sound of a car door slamming prompted Sherry to get up from the sofa and go to the front door. She sighed in relief as she saw Clint's car. She watched him as he walked around to the back of the car and opened the trunk.

The late-afternoon sun played on his dark hair, pulling forth highlights of deep mahogany. Clint was one of the few men she knew who wore a uniform well. The dark-brown slacks fit his long legs and lean hips as if tailor-made just for him. The tan shirt stretched taut across his broad shoulders as he reached into the car trunk and withdrew what appeared to be the wooden parts of a crib.

She knew she should go out and help him with the load, but she still harbored a touch of resentment that he'd managed to involve her in this whole situation. He'd manipulated their friendship and her genuine caring for him, and she was—exactly where she didn't want to be.

However, her irritation with him didn't stop her from opening the door for him as he stepped up on the front porch.

"Where did you get that?" she asked as he maneuvered the wooden railings and child-size mattress through the door and into the living room.

"Etta Mae let me borrow it." He leaned the pieces against the wall and threw a smile in Kathryn's direction. "I've got more stuff out there," he said. "Be right back."

Once again she watched as he raced back out to the car. He waved at one of his neighbors, then opened the back car door and pulled out several plastic shopping bags.

As he walked back toward the house, Sherry wondered what it was that had kept him single all these years. He was a handsome man, with clean-cut features and blue eyes that promised intelligence and humor. He was considered the major catch of Armordale, yet rarely dated and had never come close to marriage other than with her.

"Etta Mae made me a list of things I'd need," he said when he was back in the house and unloading the shopping bags.

Etta Mae was the fifty-six-year-old woman who worked as a dispatcher at the sheriff's office. She was combination co-worker, mother and confidante to the men she worked with, calling out codes and procedure with the same confidence she offered wisdom and advice.

"Rice cereal, baby food, more diapers..." He crouched and pulled each item from the bags and placed them on the floor next to him. "Rattles, teething ring, sleepers."

Sherry eyed the array of items. "This doesn't look like a two-week stay," she observed.

Clint stood and shrugged. "Babies require a lot of stuff." He pulled the last item from the bag, a stuffed white bear with a bright pink bow.

"Ah, yes, that definitely looks like a must," she observed dryly.

He shrugged again and smiled sheepishly. "I couldn't resist." His blue eyes danced with pleasure as he set the soft bear next to Kathryn.

Of course he couldn't resist, Sherry thought with a pang to her heart. Every daddy should buy their daughter their first teddy bear. "I already ate supper and fed her. Her diaper has just been changed so she shouldn't need anything for a little while. Since you're home now, I'll go unpack and get settled into the spare room.''

He looked at her in surprise, his dark brows pulling together. "You already ate? I thought maybe we'd, you know, eat dinner together."

"You can't fool me, Clint Graham," she replied as she picked up the baby paraphernalia from the floor. "You assumed you would come home to a nice, home-cooked meal—a meal I would have slaved over all afternoon." She grinned at him knowingly. "I always suspected you harbored a latent streak of chauvinism in your heart."

He laughed and raised his hands in surrender. "All right. I'll confess, I did have a little fantasy of walking in this evening and smelling the savory scent of dinner cooking. As I remember, you used to make a mean hamburger casserole."

"That was a long time ago. I don't do much cooking anymore." Sherry carried the teddy bear and other items into the kitchen, aware of Clint trailing behind her. "I'm here to take care of the baby while you're at work," she said as she placed the baby food in the cabinet. "But I'm not here to take care of you."

"I know. I'm sorry," he said, his voice ringing with sincerity. "And I do appreciate what you're doing for me...and for Kathryn." He said the baby's name with a lilt in his tone, a tone that told her he'd not only accepted the possibility that Kathryn was his but considered it probable.

As Sherry placed the last of the items in the cabinet, Kathryn let loose a wail from the living room. Sherry turned and looked at Clint. "I'm officially off duty. I'll be in my room if you need me."

Without waiting for his reply, she left the kitchen, went down the hallway and into the spare room. She closed the door and leaned against it for a moment, conflicting emotions bubbling inside her.

Baby beds and baby food. Rattles and stuffed bears. They were all things she'd put behind her, wishes that belonged to another woman, a lifetime ago.

She shoved herself away from the door and unpacked the few articles of clothing she'd brought. It's not Clint's fault, a little voice niggled inside her. And it isn't Kathryn's fault. Neither of them had manufactured the situation, yet Sherry had been subtly punishing them both from the moment she'd reluctantly agreed to help Clint out.

She finished unpacking her few toiletries, then sank down on the edge of the bed. Clint's baby. It's what Sherry had wanted for him. It was why she'd broken their engagement years before. She'd wanted him to have all the things she'd never have...like babies.

If the baby did belong to Candy, then what on earth would possess the woman to leave her on Clint's doorstep with nothing but a vague note?

Of course, in Candy's case the dire circumstances might be anything from a jealous wife after her hide, to the lure of a Caribbean cruise, where a small child would cramp her style.

In any case she was once again brought back to the fact that none of this was Clint's fault. When he'd asked for her help, she'd had the option of giving it or not. She'd chosen to be here, but so far had acted rather poorly.

She stood, deciding an apology was in order. Before she could reach the door to leave the room, a knock sounded. "I'm sorry to bother you," Clint said when she opened the door.

He'd changed out of his uniform and was now clad in a pair of worn jeans and a navy T-shirt. "Could you help me put the crib together? It would be easier with two people instead of one." He held up a screwdriver and a pair of pliers.

"Of course," she agreed. "Where are you going to set it up?" she asked as they went back into the living room.

"Uh..." He frowned a moment, thinking. "I guess in my bedroom. If you'll grab Kathryn, I'll carry all the parts in there."

"Okay," Sherry agreed. She swooped the baby up in her arms, drawing in a deep breath of baby fragrance. The scent created a blend of joy and torment inside her.

Clint's large bedroom was a study in masculinity. A navy spread adorned the king-size bed, and a heavy, dark-wood double dresser took up much of the length of one wall. Scenic pictures of trout streams adorned the walls. A wooden mallard duck with a scooped-out back for pocket change sat on the dresser amid a variety of cologne bottles.

Clint carried the baby-bed parts to the empty space in front of the single window the room contained. Sherry placed the baby on her back in the center of the bed, where Kathryn cooed and aahed, perfectly satisfied to once again find her toes.

"Clint, I'm sorry I've been a jerk," Sherry said as she held the crib's side panel against the foot rail.

He smiled, the familiar gesture that created attractive sunbursts of lines at the corners of his eyes. "Beggars can't be choosers. I'd rather have a cranky Sherry than no Sherry at all."

His smile faded, and he covered her hand with his own. She'd always loved his hands. Big, strong, capable hands, his all but engulfed her smaller one. "I am grateful for your help, Sherry. I meant what I said earlier this morning. I wouldn't want to trust her to anyone but you."

The warmth of his hand on hers seemed to seep up her arm, across her body to embrace her heart. It was not the warmth of a friendly touch, but rather something deeper, more provocative.

She averted her gaze from his, confused by the strange heat that suffused her. She breathed a sigh of relief as he removed his hand from hers and picked up the screwdriver and got to work.

"Did Walt give you a hard time about taking off work?" he asked as his long fingers nimbly placed a brass screw in the appropriate place.

"Walt doesn't know how to do anything but give me a hard time," she replied.

Clint laughed. "He's the biggest curmudgeon this town has ever known. I've never seen a man who takes such misery in each and every day."

Sherry's laughter joined his as she thought of her boss at the bar. "If Walter isn't moaning, he's whining." She picked up the second railing and held it in place for him.

Clint paused and looked at her, his eyes searching hers. "Don't you ever miss teaching?" he asked.

She felt the barrier fall into place, the self-protective wall that kept her from feeling the emotions of the woman she'd once been...and would never be again. "Never," she replied more sharply than she intended. She forced a light smile. "I love working at the bar. I love the nighttime hours, all the people I meet, and I make a pretty decent wage with tips." She raised her chin a notch, as if defying him to say anything to the contrary.

Clint studied her for a long moment, then nodded and went back to work.

Within a few more minutes the crib was together and the mattress was in place. Sherry placed the sheets Etta Mae had sent with Clint on the mattress as Clint picked up the little girl from the bed.

"I'm going to fry a couple of hamburger patties," he said as they left his bedroom. "Sure you don't want something to eat?"

"No, I'm fine. I was up late last night, and I'm exhausted. If you don't mind, I think I'll just call it a day."

She didn't want to sit in the kitchen and watch Clint cook while the baby cooed and kicked in her car seat. It felt too intimate, too domestic.

"Towels are under the sink in the bathroom, and if you need anything else, just ask," he replied. He looked so darned handsome standing there, the tools in one hand, the baby in his arms.

"I'm sure I'll be fine," Sherry replied. "I'll see you in the morning," she added, then turned on her heels and headed for her room.

She grabbed her nightgown and robe, then went into the bathroom, intent on a nice long shower to ease the tension that had tugged at her back and shoulders all day.

She hadn't lied when she'd told Clint she was exhausted. She'd worked until after three the night before, then his phone call had awakened her at just a few minutes after seven. She usually required at least eight hours of sleep to function properly.

As she stood beneath the hot spray of the shower, she thought again of that moment when Clint's hand had covered hers.

For just a brief moment she'd remembered when the touch of his hand had made her knees weaken, her breath catch in her throat. She'd remembered how Clint's touch, his kiss, had made it so difficult for her to keep her vow to be a virgin bride.

Definitely a lack of sleep, she decided. Those days of romance and chemistry were long gone where they were concerned.

She took an unusually long shower, relaxing muscle by muscle beneath the warm water. When she finally finished, she dried off and slipped into her nightclothes, then eased the bathroom door open. The scent of cooked hamburger hung in the air, and she assumed enough time had elapsed that Clint had already finished eating.

As she started to open the door to her bedroom, she heard the faint murmur of his deep voice coming from the living room. She peeked around the corner of the hallway and saw Clint sitting on the sofa, Kathryn snuggled against his chest.

"Sweet little baby girl, I'm right here for you. I'm right here and I'm not going anywhere." His voice was softer than Sherry had ever heard it, a deep, melodic singsong of love. His hand stroked the top of the baby's head, lulling her to sleep.

This was what it could have been, she thought, as fantasies danced through her head. She could easily imagine herself on the sofa, a baby in her arms, both of them surrounded by Clint's strong embrace.

She blinked to erase the deceptive image, her vision blurring with a trace of tears. A fool's fantasy, that's what it was.

She backed away and retreated to her room, swallowing against the tears that still threatened. She'd always known Clint would make a wonderful father, and the scene she'd just witnessed attested to that fact. Already his heart was embracing the child he thought to be his.

Yes, it's what she'd always wanted for him, but having Kathryn here, seeing Clint and the baby together, had stirred up emotions Sherry had believed were behind her. She'd thought she could handle it, but it was too much.

First thing in the morning she had to tell Clint that she couldn't help him anymore. As much as she cared for Clint, as much as she would like to be here for him, she had to protect her own heart.

Chapter Three

Clint groggily opened one eyelid, vaguely wondering if he'd fallen asleep the night before with the television on. No...he wasn't on the sofa. He was in bed, and the noise that had awakened him wasn't the television.

As the last of sleep fell away and consciousness overtook him, he sat up and realized exactly what the sound was that had awakened him from his slumber.

Kathryn. She lay on her back, arms waving and legs flailing. Her hands opened and closed as if in an attempt to capture the pale light of dawn that seeped through the window.

Although she wasn't fussing at the moment, she'd been up and down all night. And consequently so had Clint.

At midnight he'd given her a bottle and changed her diaper. At two o'clock he'd sat next to the crib and stroked her cheek until she'd fallen back to sleep. At three he'd rocked her in his arms and sung her every lullaby that had not been sung to him as a child.

Although it was early and Clint felt the weariness of too little sleep, he also felt the profound joy of fatherhood. With each and every moment that passed he was more and more certain that Kathryn was his.

He wasn't sure why Candy hadn't told him, didn't know what kind of game she might be playing, but if it was a ploy to gain support, both emotionally and financially from him, that wasn't a problem.

Clint intended to be a father in every sense of the word to the little girl. He'd pay support and demand liberal visitation. If he discovered that Candy wasn't a fit mother, then he'd fight her in court for full custody. But first he had to find out exactly what was going on. And that meant he had to get up out of bed.

He rolled out of bed, pulled on a pair of jeans, then walked over to the side of the crib. Kathryn smiled. Like a ray of sunshine, the toothless gesture warmed him through and through. Kathryn. His child. His daughter.

"Hi, sweetheart," he said, and touched a finger to her cheek. "Are you ready for a diaper change?"

She kicked her legs, as if urging him to hurry. "Okay...okay." He changed her diaper, then picked her up and carried her into the kitchen.

The minute he placed her in the car seat she started to fuss, and he knew it was probably hunger. He moved quickly to make her a bottle, then propped it up with a dish towel so she could drink while he made a necessary pot of coffee.

He wondered if Sherry was up yet. He hadn't heard any noise from her room as he'd walked past it. He knew she was accustomed to keeping odd hours because of her waitressing job. But she'd gone to bed the night before at a ridiculously early hour.

Clint looked at the clock on the stove. It was just a few minutes before six. He'd give Sherry an hour or so, then he would need to wake her up so he could get ready for work.

A moment later he poured himself a cup of coffee and sat down at the kitchen table, his head filled with thoughts of the woman who slept in his spare room.

Normally there was very little awkwardness between them, but since she'd arrived to help him out with Kathryn, there had been a strange energy between them...one he wasn't sure he understood.

He only knew one thing. He would never want to do anything to jeopardize the friendship they'd managed to develop when they'd outgrown their case of puppy love. They'd only been twenty-three and it had been a first serious relationship for both of them.

Puppy love. Was that what it had been? What he and Sherry had shared? He'd told himself often in the past five years that that's what it must have been—an innocent first love that couldn't sustain itself outside childish fantasy.

However, at the time he'd been in it, it hadn't felt childish or fanciful at all. Loving Sherry had consumed him. Planning for their future together had filled his life with a happiness and contentment he'd never known before or since. But it was done, a part of the past he rarely took out to examine.

She'd chosen not to be with him, insisted that her love for him had changed, and nothing she'd said or done in the intervening years had indicated anything different. She'd made her choice where he was concerned, and she seemed satisfied with that choice. End of story.

By the time he finished his cup of coffee, Kathryn had taken most of her bottle and had fallen back asleep. He checked the clock once again and realized he needed to get Sherry up.

He poured another cup of coffee, added two scoops of sugar and a liberal splash of milk, just the way Sherry liked it. Carrying the cup, he walked down the hallway to her closed door.

He rapped his knuckles gently against the wood, then waited for a reply. Nothing. No sound of stirring, no sound of anything remotely alive on the other side of the door. He knocked louder.

"Yes..." The sleepy reply drifted out, and Clint took it as encouragement to go in.

The moment he opened the door, he realized his mistake. She sat up and grabbed the sheet to her chest, but not before he saw the dainty spaghetti straps of her burgundy nightgown, not before he'd seen the expanse of creamy skin, the swell of her breasts barely hidden by the silky material.

Heat flooded through him. Unexpectedly. Spontaneously. He felt as if he'd been plunged into a fiery inferno.

"Uh...I brought you coffee," he said, then cleared his throat in embarrassment. The room seemed smaller than it ever had before, and he felt as if somehow the air had gotten thicker, more difficult to breath.

"Thanks...you can just put it there." She gestured to the top of the dresser, then ran one hand self-consciously through her short hair.

He nodded and set the cup down, conscious of the flowery scent of the room—a delicate, feminine fragrance he'd always associated with Sherry. "Uh...I've got to get ready for work in just a few minutes," he said, looking not directly at her but at some undefinable point over her head.

"Okay...just give me a minute or two and I'll be out." She didn't look at him, either, but rather kept her gaze carefully schooled just to his left.

He escaped the room and went back into the kitchen. He eased himself into a chair at the table and took in a deep breath. Slowly he inhaled and exhaled, waiting for the warmth suffusing him to cool.

His mind filled with her vision…soft. She'd looked softer, more vulnerable than he'd seen her in years. Her features had been relaxed, the morning sun painting them in golden hues.

Her hair had been mussed, her eyes drowsy pools of forest-green. She'd looked warm and cozy and sexy as hell, and for a moment he'd wanted to shuck his jeans and climb into bed with her.

He'd wanted to touch the soft skin that had momentarily been exposed to his gaze, had wanted to cup her breasts in his hands as he molded the length of her body against his.

He shoved his chair back and stood, the sudden movement and scrape of the chair against the floor startling Kathryn, who opened her mouth and bellowed in protest. "Hey…hey." He leaned over the little girl in an effort to comfort her. "It's all right. I'm sorry I scared you."

In truth, he'd scared himself with those crazy thoughts about Sherry. Apparently it had been far too long since he'd been with a woman, he told himself. Since Candy. A year and a half. It had been a year and a half since he'd made love. No wonder he'd momentarily entertained crazy, sexual thoughts about Sherry.

As if the baby felt the tension ebbing from him, her cries halted. At that moment Sherry entered the kitchen, coffee cup in hand.

She was clad in a pair of jeans and an oversize peach-colored T-shirt. Her hair was neatly combed and her face appeared to be freshly scrubbed. "One more cup of coffee and I'll almost feel human," she said as she made her way toward the coffeepot.

He smiled, feeling as if they were back on normal footing. "You don't drink coffee," he teased. "You drink coffee-flavored sugar and milk."

"That's the only way I can tolerate this sludge you call coffee," she returned with a smile.

"I've got to get showered and dressed. Andy will be here in a little while to pick me up." He headed for the door.

"Clint?"

He turned back to her. She looked at him, then at the baby, then back to him, her brow furrowed in thought. "Never mind," she finally said.

"Everything all right?" he asked.

She nodded. "Everything is fine. Go get ready for work."

A moment later, as Clint stood beneath the spray of the shower, he wondered if she'd intended to leave. Had she stopped him to tell him to get somebody else to help him out?

If that had been the case, she'd apparently changed her mind, and for that he was grateful. Clint had no idea what he'd do if Sherry decided she didn't want to be here, didn't want to help him with Kathryn.

He had no brothers or sisters, and his parents were dead. Well, dead as far as he was concerned.

Funny, he rarely thought about the people who had raised him. They hadn't been a big part of his life when he was growing up and needed them, and they certainly hadn't tried to be a part of his life when he'd reached the age of adulthood.

He shut off the shower and grabbed a towel. He didn't know if Sherry had intended to tell him she wanted out. He also had no idea what had caused the crazy thoughts he'd entertained about her moments before.

Sherry'd had every intention of telling him to find somebody else to watch Kathryn. She'd gone to sleep the night before determined to tell Clint first thing this morning that she was leaving, going back to her own life, where babies didn't exist and heartache didn't happen.

So, what had happened to her intentions? She sipped her coffee and frowned thoughtfully, her gaze lingering on the baby. Was it because in the light of day she felt stronger, better able to cope with the entire situation?

Or was it already too late—her heart was already entangled with the blue-eyed cherubic face that offered her a drooling, toothless smile? She smiled back at Kathryn, who kicked her legs and waved her arms in response.

"In for a penny, in for a pound," Sherry said aloud, then moved away from the baby as she heard a knock on the front door. That would be Andy to pick up Clint.

She opened the front door to admit the overweight, baby-faced deputy. "Hi, Andy," she said. "Come on in. Clint will be ready in a few minutes."

Andy looked down at the two foam coffee cups he held in his hand. He offered her one of them, but she shook her head. "I've got coffee in the kitchen."

Andy followed her through the living room and into the kitchen, exclaiming in delight as Kathryn offered him a gurgle and a smile. "Isn't she just the sweetest little thing," he said. He set the cups down, then held out a finger, and Kathryn's tiny hand reached out and latched on.

"Can I?" He gestured to pick her up.

"Be my guest," Sherry said, knowing the big man was as gentle as they came.

"She was sleeping yesterday morning when I was here," he explained as he unbuckled her from the car seat and carefully lifted her into his arms. "Isn't she a dandy." His voice was soft with awe.

Kathryn grabbed his nose with one hand, an ear with the other, contorting his face into a comic mask. Sherry laughed, and at that moment Clint walked in.

He looked at his deputy and shook his head with a wry grin. "And to think he's almost all that stands between the good people of Armordale and the criminals."

Sherry laughed again and rescued Andy by taking the little girl in her arms. Her laughter faltered, and she gazed at Clint. "I'll tell you what's criminal—leaving a baby on a doorstep with nothing more than a note for company. What if you hadn't been home? What if you'd been out of town on a trip or something?"

Sherry closed her mouth. She'd obviously surprised Clint and Andy with her outburst, but she'd surprised herself more.

She'd been thinking these things, but hadn't intended to say them out loud. It didn't seem fair that she could never have children, yet somebody who'd had this precious little girl had left her like a newspaper on a porch.

"I'm sorry." She felt the stain of embarrassment that covered her face. "It's really none of my business."

"Nonsense," Clint objected. "Of course it's your business. I made it yours when I asked for your help. And you're absolutely right. I tried to call Candy several times yesterday and got no answer. Then I got sidetracked with a robbery case and gathering up the things the baby would need while she was here.''

"Who got robbed?'' Sherry asked curiously. There was very little crime in Armordale and normally a robbery would be big news.

"Jerry Baker's convenience store was robbed of four pieces of bubblegum and two candy bars. We caught the culprits, two eight-year-olds who had decided to skip school and got hungry around noon.'' Clint picked up one of the foam cups Andy had carried in.

Andy smiled at Sherry. "Those two boys will think twice about even entering a store after the lecture Clint gave them.'' He picked up his cup and looked at Clint expectantly. "Are you ready?''

Clint nodded, then looked at Sherry. "I'll have some answers when I get home this evening.'' He reached out and brushed Kathryn's cheek with one finger. Her mouth popped open as if he was offering her a bottle. They all laughed, and then the men left for their day at work.

When they had gone, Sherry sank down at the table to drink another cup of coffee, her gaze lingering on Kathryn, who'd fallen back asleep and was once again safely ensconced in the car seat.

If Clint found Candy today, then it was probable she would return to collect her child...if Kathryn was Candy's. Sherry was aware that there was a possibility Kathryn didn't belong to Candy, but the possibility seemed slim.

The timing was right for Kathryn to be Clint and Candy's child, and the whole thing smelled of Candy's manipulation. It was possible Candy had left the baby here with Clint so he'd bond with her, then Candy could reappear for a happy family reunion and snag Clint into marriage…something she hadn't been able to do fifteen months before.

Clint's marriage to any woman would forever change the dimensions of his friendship with Sherry. She knew no wife would want her hanging around, buddying with the handsome sheriff. And Sherry knew Clint had a strong sense of what was morally and ethically right. Despite the fact that he didn't love Candy, he'd marry her if he thought that was what was best for their child. And Sherry would lose him forever.

She got up from the table and moved to the window. Staring outside, she fought against a wave of profound sadness, struggled to stop the wind of abiding loneliness that blew through her.

If that happened, when Clint eventually married, it wasn't as though Sherry would be losing her one true love. She chided herself. Friendships came and went, developed by fate, and if fate decreed that Clint and Sherry's friendship fall away, then so be it.

After all, Sherry had already managed to deal with the loss of her hopes, her dreams. Surely when the time came, she'd deal with the loss of Clint in her life just as efficiently.

As with the day before, the hours passed quickly. When Kathryn awakened from her nap, Sherry fed her some rice cereal and baby fruit, then bathed her in the kitchen sink and placed her in one of the new little sleepers Clint had brought home.

She tried desperately to remain emotionally uninvolved, to take care of the child without any real affection creeping into her heart. But it was impossible. Like a child of magic, Kathryn spun an enchanted spell of love that touched all who came near her.

With a sinking feeling in her heart, Sherry had to accept that she was no exception. With every minute that passed she was falling more and more in love with the little girl.

Clint punched in Candy's phone number for the fifth time that day, frowning as the phone on the other end of the line rang and rang with no reply. Candy had always had an answering machine, but no machine clicked on for the caller to leave a message.

"Clint?" Andy poked his head into Clint's tiny office. "Betty Wade is on the phone. She wants to know how much trouble she'll get into if she shoots Walt Clary's dog."

Clint hung up the phone receiver. "Why does she want to shoot Walt's dog?" he asked, although he suspected he knew the answer.

"Seems the dog comes to visit each morning and

digs up her flower beds. You know how Betty is about those flowers of hers.''

Clint nodded. ''Tell her if she shoots Walt's dog, then I'll have to arrest her, and I don't think she'd like our accommodations here.''

Andy disappeared from Clint's doorway only to reappear a moment later. ''She wants to know if she shoots Walt will you arrest her or give her a medal for the good deed?''

Clint laughed. ''I'll talk to her.'' He punched the lit button on his phone. ''Betty, Sheriff Graham here. You and Walt having problems again?''

He listened to the older woman rant and rave about her neighbor and his dog. ''I'll run by Walt's and have a talk with him,'' he promised. ''And you promise me you'll keep that shotgun packed away.''

He hung up and stood, stretching out the kinks the morning of sitting had brought. He left his office, told Andy and Etta Mae he was driving out to Walt's, then got into the patrol car and headed toward the small farmhouse on the edge of town where Walter Clary lived.

As he drove, his thoughts drifted to that early-morning moment when he'd walked into Sherry's bedroom. He'd been fighting all day to keep the vision out of his head, but without much success.

If Clint were honest with himself, he'd acknowledge that there had been times over the past five years when he'd had sexual thoughts about Sherry.

They had been fleeting fantasies, lasting only mere seconds and easily put into a secret place in his mind.

But actually seeing her in that bed, imagining her sweet, sleepy-body warmth and catching a glimpse of her creamy breasts, had stirred emotions he'd thought he'd long ago left behind, where she was concerned.

He rolled down the window, welcoming the floral-scented spring air that flowed into the car. He had to halt any fantasy he had about Sherry.

He valued her friendship, knew that after the flare of passion, in the morning light after darkest desire, they would still be left with the fact that he hadn't been enough for her. And he feared a foray into the forbidden territory of passion would destroy any hope for friendship between them.

No, better to keep reminding himself that he and Sherry hadn't been right as lifetime partners for each other, however if he kept his head, they could be lifetime friends.

He slowed as he drove past Betty Wade's small house. As usual, this time of year always brought with it a profusion of color to her yard. Flowers in a vast array of colors and varieties filled a dozen beds.

Betty's flowers were her family, and he understood her frustration over Walt's wayward mutt, who every year seemed to make it his personal doggy business to dig up each and every member of Betty's "family."

He checked his watch as he pulled up in front of Walt's small, untidy house. It was just a few minutes after three. Walt usually didn't go down to the tavern until about five.

As Clint got out of the car, Walt stepped out of his front door, the little one-eared mongrel at his side. "I knew she'd be calling the law," Walt exclaimed before Clint could say anything. "That woman's got a mouth as big as this state."

"You know we've got a leash law, Walt," Clint said, trying to maintain a look of stern authority. "I'd hate to lock up Rover."

"Rover don't mean no harm." Walt reached down and stroked the dog behind his one ear. "He's got one of them flower fetishes...can't help himself. You ought to lock up Betty, she's meaner than Rover would ever dream of being."

It was the same battle every spring and summer, and Clint had a feeling the two older adults got a perverse satisfaction from their neighborly bickering.

"I'm mad at you, anyways," Walt continued. "You stole my best waitress, got her baby-sitting from what I hear." He cast Clint a sly smile. "Hear tell that baby just might be yours."

"You shouldn't be listening to gossip," Clint replied. "And I only stole Sherry for a few days."

Walt snorted. "A few days of housewifing and

nursemaiding and you really think she'll want to come back to my stinking bar?''

He shook his head, his features tugged downward in misery. ''She probably won't be back. She'll be wanting to get married and start her own family, now that you gave her a taste of that sort of thing. Without her at the bar, business will drop off. I'll probably have to sell the place.''

Clint let him ramble on and when the old man paused for breath Clint jumped in. ''It's not working, Walt. You can change the subject all you want, you can blame me for all the miserable days you think are ahead of you, but I still remember the reason I'm here. Keep that dog on a leash and out of Betty's flowers or I'll have to fine you and arrest Rover.''

Without waiting for Walt's reply, Clint strode back to his patrol car and got in. Minutes later as he headed back to the station, his mind worked over what Walt had said about Sherry.

''She'll be wanting to get married and start her own family.''

Of course, Walt wouldn't know that wasn't possible for Sherry. There would be no family for her unless she married a man who already had children.

He hoped that happened some day for her. He hoped she met a wonderful man, who had lovely small children who needed her. He wanted her to be happy and had long ago realized that she didn't believe her happiness could ever be with him.

He knew she dated occasionally, but she never discussed her personal relationships with him and in any case, she never seemed to date any one man for very long.

Yes, he wanted her to be happy. What he didn't understand is why the thought of Sherry, happy and married to another man, caused such a cold wind of loneliness to blow through him.

Chapter Four

"I can't figure out why I can't get hold of Candy," Clint said as he helped Sherry clear the supper dishes. Sherry had surprised him and cooked a roast and potatoes. The scent had filled the house throughout the afternoon, reminding Sherry of childhood Sundays, when her mother had cooked roasts for after-church meals.

"The note said Kathryn's mother would be away for a while," Sherry reminded him. "Maybe she left on a trip." She turned on the taps to fill the sink full of soapy water. "It makes sense that she dropped the baby here, knowing you'd take care of Kathryn while she went off on a jaunt. Maybe all the danger and intrigue stuff was just for fun." Sherry tried to keep her voice devoid of censure.

Clint stared thoughtfully at the baby, who occupied her place of honor in the car seat in the center of the table. "I don't know. I realize Candy is selfish and vain, but I just can't see her being self-centered enough to abandon her child on my porch."

Sherry plunged the silverware and glasses into the soapy water, biting her tongue. She hadn't liked Candy from the moment Clint had introduced her. Nobody had been happier than Sherry when Clint and Candy's relationship had ended.

But was it really over? Kathryn might possibly be the bond that would forever tie the two of them together—a bond Sherry couldn't compete with.

She scrubbed the glasses with a vengeance, silently chiding herself. Of course she couldn't compete with Candy's ability to bear children, and she certainly didn't want to compete with Candy for Clint.

"I'm going to try to call her again right now," Clint said. "I've been calling her during work hours, but she's got to be home sooner or later." He walked over to the phone on the counter and picked up the receiver.

As he punched in the numbers to make the call, Sherry tried to ignore how attractive he looked in his jeans and white T-shirt. Had his shoulders always been so broad? The cotton material of the shirt tugged and stretched across his back as he reached out to chuck Kathryn beneath her chin.

And why, oh, why was she noticing the breadth

of his shoulders, his taut buttocks, his lean hips? For the past few years, she'd managed to transform Clint in her mind from a virile, sexy man to an asexual friend. Why on earth was he suddenly changing back to the desirable man he'd once been?

She rinsed the glasses and placed them in the dish drainer, then dunked the plates in the sinkful of water. At the same time Clint hung up the phone with a sigh of frustration. "I just don't get it. Not even an answering machine picks up," he exclaimed.

"Maybe you should try information," Sherry suggested. She dried her hands and turned to face him, vaguely surprised that he hadn't been more aggressive in searching for Candy.

He stood next to the table, staring at the baby. The expression on his face was one of love. He'd once looked at Sherry with that same expression. The memory sent a shaft of pain shooting through her, a heartache she desperately shoved aside.

"Isn't it possible Candy has moved, that the number you have for her isn't hers any longer?" Sherry continued. "After all, it's been almost a year and a half since you last spoke to her."

"Maybe you're right. I'll try information and see what I can find out." Once again he picked up the phone and punched in the appropriate numbers.

As he spoke to an operator, Sherry finished up the last of the dishes, then poured herself a cup of coffee and sat at the table.

She wondered if Clint was dragging his feet about actively pursuing the mystery of Kathryn's parentage because he'd gotten caught up in a father fantasy.

Clint had told her at one time that he'd never thought much of having children, that being a father just wasn't that important to him. But that had been before Kathryn's presence in his life. He'd been transformed since Kathryn—transformed from a man who hadn't thought about having children to a father.

"You're right," Clint said as he hung up the receiver. "That number I had for Candy is no longer a working number, and they don't have a new listing for her." He sat at the table and raked a hand through his hair in frustration.

"So, what are you going to do now?" Sherry asked.

"I don't know. I can't remember the name of the travel agency Candy was working at when I met her, and there's got to be a hundred travel agencies in Kansas City."

"We could divide them up, spend the day tomorrow calling each one," Sherry offered.

Clint's frown deepened. "It sounds like a lot of time and work with little possibility for success. If I remember correctly, Candy hated her job and was talking about making a career change. It's very possible she isn't working for a travel agency any longer."

Sherry got up to refill her coffee cup. "Want a cup?" she offered.

"Sure. Thanks." He flashed her a smile that sent warmth through her. "By the way, I don't think I mentioned that your pot roast was exceptional."

She grinned as she placed his cup before him, then rejoined him at the table. "You're just saying that so I'll be buttered up enough to cook again tomorrow night."

He laughed and reached out to cover her hand with his. "Sherry, I don't expect you to cook or clean for me." The laughter faded from his eyes and the blue appeared to deepen. "I know these past two days with Kathryn have been difficult on you, and I'll never be able to repay you for what you're doing for me."

Escape. Sherry's mind sounded the alarm. His hand over hers was far too warm, the gaze of his eyes achingly soft. All combined to evoke a wistful desire for him to take her in his arms—a desire to taste his lips and see if the sweet memory of their past kisses was accurate.

"Friends help friends," she said as she eased her hand out from his. She stood, needing to distance herself physically from his overwhelming masculine presence. "If you don't mind, I thought maybe I'd take a walk and get a little fresh air. I've been cooped up inside for the past two days and I'd like to stretch my legs a little."

"Sounds like a great idea. Do you mind if we tag along?"

Yes, I mind, she wanted to scream. I need some time alone, time to put you back where you belong...in the darkest recesses of my mind. "But you don't have a stroller or anything," she protested.

Clint shrugged, then stood and unbuckled Kathryn from the car seat. "She doesn't weigh more than a peanut. I can just carry her. Besides," he gestured with one arm toward the window. "It's an absolutely gorgeous evening, perfect for a leisurely walk."

Sherry nodded and swallowed a sigh of resignation.

Within minutes the three of them stepped out of Clint's home and into the warm evening. Sherry breathed deeply of the fresh air, welcoming a scent devoid of baby powder and earthy, men's cologne.

"Left or right?" Clint asked as they reached the end of his walkway and stepped onto the sidewalk.

How about I go left and you and Kathryn go right? She shrugged, wishing she had the nerve to tell him that he bothered her for some reason this evening.

Hot and bothered, that's how she felt, and it disturbed her, threatened the peace she'd finally made within herself over the past five years.

"Let's go left," Clint decided.

For a few minutes they walked in silence, the

only sound Kathryn's happy cooing and the noise of a town readying itself for the night. Garage doors closed, and lights appeared in homes, beams of illumination against the falling twilight.

For some reason the noises and the sight of families reuniting at the end of a day filled Sherry with a wistful yearning. Would she ever have somebody to share her evenings with?

"Maybe I should call Stan Glenaire," Clint said, breaking the silence that had lengthened between them.

"If anyone can find Candy, I'm sure Stan can," Sherry replied agreeably.

Stan Glenaire was an old friend of Clint's from when Clint had lived in Kansas City. He'd worked for fifteen years as a police officer on the Kansas City force, then had decided to become a private investigator.

About once a month Stan drove from Kansas City to the small town of Armordale to have dinner with Clint. Sherry had joined them several times and enjoyed the tall, attractive P.I., who had a devilish sense of humor and a kind, giving heart.

"I'll call Stan first thing in the morning and see what he can find out for me." He shifted Kathryn from one arm to the other. "I spoke to Walt today. He's sure you aren't coming back to work for him."

She looked at Clint in surprise. "Why would he think that?"

''He figures now that you've had a taste of being a housewife, you'll want to get married and not be a waitress anymore.''

Sherry laughed, although the sound lacked any real humor. ''He doesn't have to worry about that. I have absolutely no plans to marry anyone.''

''Ever?'' His gaze bore into hers.

She looked away, unable to sustain his intense scrutiny. ''I don't know…ever is a long time. All I really know is that my life is full and happy right now.''

''Don't you ever get lonely?'' he asked, his voice soft and searching.

''Sometimes,'' she conceded. ''Although I think it would be infinitely more lonely to be married to somebody I didn't love.'' Infinitely more lonely to be married and know there would be no children for continuity, no babies to hold hope and dreams, to deepen the loving connection of parents.

''Why haven't you married, Clint?'' The words popped out of Sherry's mouth before she realized they'd been formed in her brain. She attempted to lighten the mood with a teasing smile. ''I have it on good authority that you're considered the premier catch of the county.''

He threw back his head and laughed. ''That's not saying much in a town where the average age of the male population is over sixty.'' He sobered, his gaze once again playing on her features. ''I intended to marry once, and that didn't work out. I haven't given it much thought since.''

Sherry felt her cheeks warm with a blush, and once again she looked away from him. They had never acknowledged their past, never spoken about their engagement.

She'd known she'd hurt him, but it had been a hurt necessary for his ultimate happiness.

She stopped walking. ''We should turn around and start back. It's getting dark and cooling off.'' What she really wanted was a change in conversation, a halt to the thoughts their talk had stirred.

They turned around and started back the way they'd come. Once again they walked in silence, waving to neighbors as they passed. Kathryn had fallen asleep, snuggled against Clint's chest. Each time Sherry looked at the baby, at Clint, who held her as if she were the most precious bundle in the world, a small ache renewed itself in her heart.

''How's your family doing?'' Clint asked. ''I rarely see your mom or your sister in town anymore.''

''They're fine. Mom stays busy with her work at the shop, and Susan's children keep her happy at home.'' A pang of guilt swept through Sherry.

She had allowed her relationship with her sister to fall aside once Susan began having children with regularity and ease. It had just become too painful to see her sister maternally fulfilled with four children, while Sherry would never enjoy that same kind of bliss.

"Mom is still angry with me for quitting my teaching job and going to work for Walt," she added.

"It was a surprise for everyone who knew you," Clint agreed. "You were such a marvelous teacher."

Sherry felt the barrier around her heart strengthening, becoming more dense and impenetrable. "I got tired of it. Wiping runny noses every day, dealing with immature little minds, listening to endless chatter."

Clint laughed. "Sounds to me like what you do at Walt's now."

Sherry laughed as well, genuinely tickled as she realized the truth of his words. "You're right." But he didn't understand how painful teaching had become.

He hadn't experienced a little boy pressing against his body for a hug, a little girl wrapping chubby arms around his neck. And that sweet smell of childhood that had clung to each and every child...it had been sheer torture to deal with every day and know she'd never have a little boy or girl of her own.

She'd distanced herself from everything that hurt in her life—her teaching, her family...Clint.

In many ways giving up Clint had been far more difficult that quitting her job or remaining emotionally distant from her family. In giving up Clint, she'd chosen a life devoid of love. The past two days, spending time with him, with Kathryn, had only redefined that particular pain in her heart.

As they walked back into Clint's house, he carried the sleeping baby directly to the crib in his room, then rejoined her in the living room.

"Clint, when I agreed to help you out here, it was only for a couple of days," Sherry said. "If you don't find something out tomorrow about Candy, you're going to have to find somebody else to help you. I've got to get back to my own life."

A look of sheer panic crossed his face as he joined her on the sofa. "Ah, Sherry, don't say that. I've got no control over how quickly or how slowly we find Candy." The panicked expression ebbed. "Besides, what's waiting for you at your apartment? You've got no cats, no dogs. Hell, you don't even have plants that need watering."

He reached over and smoothed a strand of her hair off her forehead, the touch strangely more intimate than any they'd shared in years. "Don't run out on us now, Sherry. Kathryn needs you, and I need you."

He leaned forward, so close she could see those bewitching silvery flecks in his blue eyes, so close she felt surrounded by his scent, his warmth.

For a brief moment she thought he might kiss her. And she wanted him to—wanted it desperately. She wanted to feel his tender lips against hers, his strong arms holding her tight. Unconsciously she leaned forward, allowing him easier access should he decide to press his mouth against hers.

He didn't. With an abrupt burst of energy he stood. "Hopefully tomorrow we'll have some answers. But if we don't, I hope you'll change your mind and stick around." He raked a hand through his hair and took another step back from the sofa. "I think maybe it'd be best if I call it a night. I should try to get some sleep while Kathryn is sleeping. I'll see you in the morning."

"Good night, Clint," Sherry said. When he left the room and she heard the sound of his bedroom door softly closing, she released a deep sigh, one that combined both disappointment and relief.

She'd wanted him to kiss her, and that scared her. She grabbed one of the throw pillows and hugged it to her breast, wondering if she squeezed it tight enough, would it allay the emptiness inside her.

She'd not only wanted Clint to kiss her. She'd wanted him to take her in his arms, caress her body until it sang with need.

Her mind filled with memories of how it had once been between them—the sweet, explosive passion they'd enjoyed, then halted, because of Sherry's desire to be a virgin on their wedding night.

She wished now she hadn't been so adamant about wanting to be a virgin bride. She wished she'd allowed their passion to sweep them beyond reason. How she wished that just once she'd allowed control to slip, allowed their heated caresses to blossom into complete lovemaking.

She hugged the pillow closer. But perhaps it was best this way, that she didn't have the memory of making love with Clint to further torment her.

Seeing him with Kathryn these past two days had simply sanctioned the decision she'd made so long ago to let him go. He deserved a loving wife and lots of babies. He deserved a whole woman, not the barren, bitter woman Sherry had become.

Clint's hands shook as he unbuttoned his jeans and kicked them off. He sank down on the edge of his bed and drew in a gulp of air.

Desire. It winged through him like tiny electrical currents sizzling inside his veins. And desire had a name…Sherry. And for just a moment, as they'd sat so achingly close on the sofa, he'd thought he'd seen the same emotion in the depths of her eyes.

He pulled his T-shirt over his head and added it to his jeans on the floor. Socks quickly followed, then he turned out the light and got into bed.

Surely he'd been mistaken. He'd imagined the desire clouding the forest-green of her eyes. He'd had too little sleep the night before and had been tired enough to fantasize things that weren't really there.

He'd survived the decision Sherry had made where he was concerned. He'd managed to live without loving her in any romantic sense for the past five years. He couldn't afford to have things change. He refused to allow a momentary flare of chemistry to destroy the friendship they'd managed to sustain.

He closed his eyes, secure that whatever emotion he'd momentarily felt, whatever he'd believed he'd seen in her eyes, hadn't been real.

Within minutes he was asleep and dreaming. He knew he was dreaming because he was once again twenty-three years old, and he and a twenty-one-year-old Sherry were parked at Armordale Lake, the small body of water on the outskirts of town. It had always been their special place to spend time alone.

Clint had an apartment, but they both spent little time there, knowing that the utter privacy of the apartment would make it easier for them to fully indulge the passion they had for each other—a passion they constantly fought against, awaiting their wedding night.

Sherry's warmth filled his arms, and he drank greedily from her lips. Her body was pliant against his as she pressed eagerly against him, trusting that he'd be the one to call a halt before things got out of control.

"Sherry, sweet Sherry," he murmured as he kissed her cheeks, the area just behind her ear, then captured her mouth with his once again.

Then suddenly she pulled away from him and got

out of the car. "Sherry!" He called after her as she ran to the water's edge.

He jumped out of the car and ran after her, unable to reach her before she walked into the water toward the center of the lake, until she disappeared from his sight, disappeared beneath the surface.

Clint didn't know if it had been the baby's cries that awakened him or his own cries. He flailed to full consciousness, Kathryn's wails filling the room.

He got out of bed and turned on the overhead light, then shook his head to rid himself of the wonderful, horrible dream.

As he changed the baby's diaper and spoke softly in an attempt to soothe her fussy cries, he tried to shove the dream images away. What remained was a terrible anguish, a hollowness in the pit of his stomach as he remembered watching Sherry disappear forever beneath the dark waters of the lake.

The fresh diaper did nothing to stop Kathryn's cries. Clint picked her up and carried her into the kitchen, where he fixed her a bottle, then returned to the bedroom.

It was just a few minutes past midnight. As he passed Sherry's room, he noticed there was no light shining from beneath the door. Apparently she was sound asleep.

He closed his door, not wanting Kathryn to awaken Sherry. He sat on the edge of the bed, the baby in his arms, and tried to feed her the bottle.

She was having nothing to do with it. She twisted

her head from side to side, evading the nipple as if the bottle contained vile medicine.

"What's the matter, sweetheart?" he asked. Giving up, he set the bottle aside and instead held her up against his chest, rocking back and forth in an effort to soothe her.

Her cries grew in pitch, becoming more shrill with each gasping breath she took. Clint didn't think it was a cry of pain, and it was obvious by the way she avoided the bottle that it wasn't a cry of hunger. So what was the matter with her?

Clint stood and began to pace, gently jiggling Kathryn up and down in his arms. Maybe she had a gas bubble or something like that. Her cries tore through him and filled him with worry. He didn't want her to cry. He wished that every day of her life, every moment of her existence, would be full of sunshine and laughter.

The door to his bedroom eased open, and Sherry appeared in the doorway. He started to give her a smile of relief, but when he saw the look in her eyes, relief fled, replaced by a stronger emotion.

In the instant she opened the door, her gaze swept the length of him, and a deep rosy hue stained her cheeks. Clint was suddenly aware of the fact that he stood before her, clad only in a pair of boxers.

The squalling baby in his arms did little to defend him against the rise of heat that began in his toes and worked its way up his body.

"I'm sorry.... I knocked, but I guess you didn't hear me," she said, her voice huskier than usual. "Having problems?" Her gaze studiously darted from one side to the other of him, never actually looking at him.

"She won't stop crying," he said. Even though he knew on an intellectual level that his boxers covered him as effectively as a bathing suit, on an emotional level the intimacy of her in her nightgown and silky robe and him in his boxers was not only working on his brain, but also on other parts of him.

Before he completely embarrassed himself, he held Kathryn out to her. "Maybe you can make her stop."

She took the baby from him, still not making eye contact with him. "You go on back to bed. You have to go to work in the morning. I'll take care of her." Without waiting for his reply, she turned and left the room.

Clint remained motionless for a long moment, waiting for his nerves, his heartbeat, his emotions to return to normal. But normalcy seemed alien to his body.

On shaky legs, he forced himself across the room to turn out the light, then crawled back into bed— a bed that suddenly felt far too cold, far too big for a single person.

He wanted Sherry. The knowledge hit him with the force of a blow to the abdomen. He'd wanted her years ago, and as impossible as it seemed, he wanted her more now.

He drew in a deep breath and allowed it to seep out of him on a wistful sigh. Nothing had changed since that time in the past when Sherry had told him she didn't want to marry him, didn't want to spend the rest of her life with him.

Turning over on his side, he realized the house had fallen silent. He could no longer hear Kathryn's wails. Apparently Sherry had worked some kind of magic and managed to soothe her.

Somehow he had a feeling Sherry wouldn't be willing to do the same for him. She wouldn't be willing to work some magic and ease the longing for her that filled his very soul.

Chapter Five

Afternoon sunlight danced through the living room curtains, carrying a pleasant warmth that increased Sherry's drowsiness. She was stretched out on the sofa, legs propped up to hold a magazine she'd been thumbing through. But her thoughts weren't on the magazine articles. She was consumed by thoughts of Clint.

Seeing him the night before in nothing but those sexy boxers had unsettled her, evoking fantasies she had no business entertaining—fantasies of her body and his, naked beneath crisp sheets, moving together in perfect unison. Sweet fantasies of his lips on hers, stealing her breath with greedy kisses, his hands stroking the length of her body as he took complete and utter possession of her.

She shook her head to dislodge such nonsense

and focused instead on thoughts of the little girl napping in Clint's bedroom.

The night before, the moment she'd taken Kathryn from Clint, the little girl had calmed down and snuggled against her. Sherry suspected she missed her mommy, and Sherry's feminine touch seemed to ease the ache of her mother's absence.

Sherry got back into bed, with Kathryn cradled in her arms. Almost instantly Kathryn fell asleep, leaving Sherry to stare at the darkness and fight her overwhelming desire for Clint.

Where had this desire come from? She'd thought she'd long ago ridden herself of any wanting of Clint. Had it only been dormant inside her, waiting for the right circumstances to make it flare up with renewed energy?

She knew better than to follow through on the desire. Nothing but heartache could come from making love to Clint. She had no future with him and making love to him would only be a temporary sort of thing at best.

She'd finally fallen into a fitful sleep. Kathryn remained sleeping peacefully in the crook of her arm through the night and awakened Sherry that morning by grasping her nose.

Closing her eyes, Sherry thought about what she'd told Clint the evening before. She'd lied when she said her life was full and happy. It wasn't. She found no pleasure in working at Walt's tavern. She hated the hours and dreaded dealing with the rowdy cowboys. She came home after working, exhausted, feet aching, but with no true fulfillment.

Maybe it was time for a change. She frowned thoughtfully. But what? What kind of changes did she want to make?

Not working at the bar these past couple of days had made her realize it was time to alter her life, but she wasn't sure exactly where to begin.

When she'd been told by the doctor she would never have children, she'd run from her job as a teacher to avoid being around children. She'd been trying to mitigate her grief, and instead had only punished herself.

She still wasn't certain that she'd be able to handle being around children all the time, but she knew for certain it was time to give Walt her notice, time for her to explore other employment options.

Frowning, she opened her eyes. An odd, barely discernible noise broke the silence of the house. She sat up and swung her legs to the floor. Nothing. She heard nothing.

She looked out the front window. Perhaps what she'd heard was a tree branch scratching against the side of the house. Her frown deepened. It couldn't be a branch blowing. Not a breath of a breeze stirred the trees.

Again the noise came…like fingernails scraping down a wall.

She stood and tilted her head to one side, attempting to identify exactly where the noise originated. Kathryn. Maybe she'd awakened from her nap and had found something to play with in her crib.

Sherry tiptoed down the hallway, pausing as she came to Clint's closed bedroom door. She shoved the door open and stepped into the room. For a moment the scene before her didn't connect in her brain. Kathryn was asleep, her bottom sticking up and her thumb in her mouth.

Behind the crib the screen on the window had been cut and was hanging. The window, which had been closed when Sherry had put Kathryn down for her nap, was now open a little more than an inch.

Sheer horror riveted her as she recognized the implications. Her initial inertia broke, and she ran to the crib and scooped up Kathryn in her arms. Ignoring Kathryn's startled cries, she slammed the window and locked it, then hurried to the front door and made sure it was securely locked.

Adrenaline still pumping, she raced into the kitchen, checked the back door to make certain it was locked, then grabbed the phone and punched in the number for the sheriff's office.

Clint answered, and at the sound of his calm, deep voice Sherry burst into tears.

"Sherry? What's wrong?" he asked urgently.

"Somebody tried to break in," she cried. "Kathryn was napping, and somebody cut the screen in your bedroom."

"What...slow down," he replied.

"Please...come home, Clint. Come home now."

He didn't reply, and it took only a moment for Sherry to realize he'd hung up. She replaced the receiver and clutched Kathryn close to her breasts.

Somebody had tried to break into the house. Why? And of all the rooms in the house, why had they chosen the one where Kathryn was sleeping, and why the window right behind her crib?

The implications terrified her. "Shh," she said softly, trying to comfort the baby, who apparently sensed Sherry's tension...her fear.

Sherry moved to the front door and peered outside. It was a beautiful spring day. Nothing looked amiss. No shadowy figures crept along the sidewalk, no car with darkly tinted windows cruised slowly past the house. And yet Sherry knew that out there was somebody who'd wanted in, somebody who'd wanted Kathryn.

She breathed a sigh of relief as she heard the distant wail of a siren. It sounded odd...the high pitched sound splitting the tranquility of the day. She couldn't remember the last time she'd heard a siren in Armordale.

A loud screech of tires signaled Clint's arrival. Sherry unlocked the front door and met him on the porch, the tears she'd thought under control once again flowing.

"Your bedroom—" She gulped, trying to get breath to tell him what had happened. "Somebody tried to break in through your bedroom window."

Clint's features were drawn taut and he looked more dangerous than she'd ever seen him. He pulled his gun from his holster. "Go inside and lock the door. Don't open it for anyone except me," he instructed.

He didn't have to tell her twice. She went back into the house, locked the door, then stood in the center of the living room. She alternated between patting Kathryn's back and swiping her own tears, which refused to stop flowing.

Kathryn's chubby little fingers curled into the cotton material of Sherry's blouse, and her sweet blue eyes gazed up at Sherry in complete and utter trust.

Sherry hugged Kathryn against her, felt the stir of maternal love well up inside her. The emotion, so rich, so pure, momentarily awed her. She'd never thought she'd feel this way.

She'd never thought she would experience loving a child to such depths, knowing she'd do whatever it took to protect the child from harm. She'd believed because she was barren that she was also devoid of any maternal instincts. But that wasn't true.

Following the awe came the grief. She loved Kathryn. In the short span of time she'd been with the little girl, Kathryn had managed to firmly wedge her way into Sherry's heart. But somewhere Kathryn had a mommy of her own, and Sherry knew her love for the child could only lead her into more heartache.

She jumped as knuckles rapped on the front door. "Sherry, it's me." Clint's voice rang out loud and clear.

She hurried to the door and unlocked it to admit him. "Did you see anyone?"

He shook his head and holstered his gun, a grim expression on his face. "Nobody. Although it's obvious somebody tried to get in through my bedroom window." He ran a hand through his hair and stared at Kathryn thoughtfully. "If you were going to break into a house to rob it, would you choose a window next to where a baby slept?"

"It depends upon whether you want to rob the house or steal the baby." Sherry spoke the words she knew they were both thinking. At the same time she tightened her grip on Kathryn, who fussed in protest and kicked to get down.

Clint's eyes darkened, and once again he looked more dangerous than Sherry had ever seen. "If this is Candy's idea of a game, I swear when I find her I'll wring her neck." The tension in his face ebbed slightly. "Here, I'll take her."

He took the wiggling baby from her arms, kissed Kathryn soundly on the forehead, then placed her on the floor and handed her a set of plastic keys that had been resting on the coffee table.

As Kathryn occupied herself cooing to the brightly colored keys, Clint took Sherry by the arm and led her to the sofa. He sank onto the cushion and pulled her down next to him.

She went willingly into the embrace he offered, needing his strong arms around her, needing the strength of his body to make her feel safe. Wrapping her arms around his neck, she buried her face into the fresh-scented cotton of his shirt.

"I was so scared," she whispered. "I opened the bedroom door and saw the screen all cut up.... If I'd waited another minute or two, Kathryn might not have been in her crib." She shuddered as a wave of horror once again swept through her.

Clint tightened his arms around her. "But you didn't wait that extra minute or two, and everything is all right. Kathryn is fine. Thank God both of you are safe and sound." He stroked a hand through her hair, then trailed a thumb down the side of her face. "Sherry." He spoke her name softly and she looked up at him.

Instantly her breath caught in her chest. He was going to kiss her. She knew it. His intention shone from his eyes, unmistakable and definite. And she had no intention of stopping him. Instead she stretched upward, giving his mouth easier access to her own.

He dipped his head and touched his lips to hers. Soft and gentle, it was a tentative kiss that instantly sparked flames inside her. Her heartbeat quickened, her pulse raced, and she opened her mouth, allowing him to deepen the kiss.

A shudder swept through his body as his tongue swirled and danced with hers. Flames of desire roared throughout her as she pressed her body more closely against his and lost herself to the internal fire his kiss stoked.

The kiss might have lasted seconds or it might have lingered for half an eternity. Sherry lost all track of time and space, of presence and self, as his mouth continued to drink from hers.

His hands moved up and down her back, pressing her breasts more firmly against his chest. She loved the feel of his solid muscles against her feminine softness.

She wanted him to hold her forever, kiss her forever. She wanted him to slowly remove her clothing and teach her about making love.

Instead he broke the kiss and abruptly stood. He moved away from the sofa before Sherry had fully registered his withdrawal from her. "I've got to take care of that window in the bedroom," he said, his voice deeper than usual.

Sherry nodded, not trusting herself to speak. Not trusting that she wouldn't beg him to come back to her, hold her through the night, make love to her until dawn crept across the sky.

As he left the house, Sherry stood on trembling legs and drew in a deep breath. She'd momentarily lost her mind. That was the only way to explain what had just occurred between them. Temporary insanity times two. They'd both lost their minds.

Their emotions, heightened by the near break-in and the sense of imminent danger, had transformed into something even more dangerous. She was grateful he'd pulled away before the momentum had become too intense to halt.

She couldn't allow such a thing to happen again. She turned and looked at Kathryn, who was happily playing with the plastic keys. She could survive the loss of Kathryn, knew the time would come when the baby would no longer be a part of her life.

But she wasn't at all sure she could survive a breakup if she fooled herself into believing she and Clint had any sort of future together. She knew the truth. There was no future for Clint with her, and she would do well to remember that.

Clint poked through the miscellaneous items in the garage, seeking a hammer and nails, trying to remember the last time he'd used either. He'd already located a large piece of plywood that would cover the bedroom window. He would board it up, and if somebody tried to get through it again, they'd have to use a chain saw.

Spying the hammer and a coffee can filled with a variety of nails, he grabbed the two items, then carried them and the plywood to the back of the house.

As he eyed the torn screen, his blood chilled and his anger rose. He was the sheriff in this town, and it seemed incredible that anyone would actually attempt to break into his home. The stakes must have been high.

Kathryn. It seemed reasonable to believe that whoever had tried to get in had been after the little girl. But why? The note that had come with Kathryn had spoken of danger. But what kind of danger? None of it made any sense.

He hefted the plywood into place and began to hammer in nails. He hoped Stan would be able to find Candy. This whole scenario smelled of her manipulation and penchant for high drama. He'd contacted Stan that morning and given him everything he knew about Candy. Hopefully Stan would have some information for him on her whereabouts in the next day or two.

Candy. He didn't know why he'd gotten involved with the woman in the first place. He'd known from the start she wasn't his type. But for the month and a half that they'd dated, she'd filled up the lonely silences in his life—the ones he'd suffered since the breakup with Sherry.

Sherry. Her name exploded in his head as he remembered the hot, eager kiss they'd shared. He began pounding in nails, using more force than necessary, hoping the expenditure of energy would somehow cause his desire for her to ebb.

He finished nailing up the plywood but was reluctant to go back inside. The lingering warmth of Sherry's kiss on his mouth made him feel vulnerable, off center.

He needed a little more time, a little space to ground himself in reality. And the reality was that Sherry was a friend, a good, valued one, but just a friend nevertheless.

He walked around the house twice more, seeking signs or clues that might help them figure out exactly what was going on, why somebody had tried to break in. But he found nothing.

The neighbors on either side were no help. The house to the left of his had nobody home. The house on the right was occupied by an elderly couple who had seen nothing and nobody suspicious.

Finally, feeling as if his wayward emotions were back in control, he went into the house. Sherry and Kathryn were in the kitchen, Sherry making coffee and Kathryn in her car seat center stage on the oak table.

"Terrific, I could use a cup of coffee," Clint said as he sat at the table. Kathryn cast him a drooling, sunshiny smile and Clint's heart expanded with love. Whoever was after her would have to come through him to get her. And that wasn't going to happen.

At this moment, as she grinned at him, he had no doubt at all that she was his. She had blue eyes, as did he. He even thought he saw a hint of his own square chin in her baby one.

She had to be his. He couldn't love her with such depth, such intensity if she weren't. It was as if his heart recognized that she was an integral part of him.

"So, what happens now?" Sherry asked as she set a cup of coffee in front of Clint, then joined him at the table with a cup of her own.

He was grateful to see nothing in her eyes except curiosity. No need, no smoldering embers of the flare of passion that had momentarily flared between them.

"There isn't much I can do to catch the person who tried to break in." He took a sip of the hot brew, then looked back at her. "You didn't see anyone at the window?"

Sherry shook her head. "Nobody. The only thing I can figure is that whoever was there saw me open the bedroom door and they ran." She frowned. "Surely you don't really think Candy is behind all this."

"There's nothing that makes me believe otherwise," Clint replied. He sighed, thinking about the woman he'd once dated. "I must have been crazy to get involved with her at all."

"You can't always control who you fall in love with," Sherry replied.

Clint attempted to swallow a burst of laughter. "Love? I didn't love Candy. Not for a minute. I didn't even like her that much."

"But then why…?" Sherry's gaze shot to Kathryn, then back to him.

"Why did I have sex with her if I didn't love

her?'' Sherry nodded, a blush coloring her cheeks. Clint took another sip of his coffee before answering.

Because I wanted to see if I could forget you. Because for three years I waited to see if you'd change your mind, waited to see if you'd ever love me again, and when I realized that wasn't going to happen, I was desperate to try to get on with my life.

So many replies danced through his head, answers he knew he wouldn't say to her. Instead he grinned wryly. ''It's possible to indulge physical pleasure without involving the head or the heart,'' he finally said.

''But why would she do something like this? Why would she leave the baby here, then manufacture an attempted kidnapping?'' Sherry asked.

''Who knows?'' Clint shrugged. ''Maybe she's trying to pay me back.''

''Pay you back for what?''

Again a wry smile leaped to his lips. ''For being able to separate body from heart, for having sex with her and not being willing to commit to her.''

He stood, uncomfortable with the entire conversation. It felt wrong, talking about having sex with another woman. ''I don't know, Sherry. Candy is the woman who put laxative in her boss's coffee when he refused to give her a raise. Who knows exactly how her mind works?''

Sherry stared at him. "She didn't. In her boss's coffee?"

He nodded. "She did. The night she told me she'd done it was the last night we went out. I didn't call her anymore, and when she called me I made excuses about work and being busy. Eventually she quit calling, and I never heard from her again."

Leaning against the refrigerator door, he sighed. "Candy had a mean streak in her. She played cruel practical jokes on people and thought they were amusing. She might be finding this whole thing with Kathryn as equally amusing."

"I can't imagine a mother finding anything remotely amusing about such a thing," Sherry said with a vengeance. "Did you talk to Stan?"

He nodded. "This morning. Hopefully he'll have something for me very soon."

Sherry leaned forward and tickled Kathryn's tummy. "Don't you worry, sweet baby. We aren't going to let anything bad happen to you," she said.

Sherry's features were softened with a lovely smile as she played with the baby. Clint watched the rise and fall of her breasts beneath her pale-pink blouse, remembered how those breasts had felt against his chest. The curve of her lips summoned her taste back to his memory, the sweet, honeyed taste of heat and desire.

Turning his back on the scene, Clint fought the

rise of renewed passion. He poured himself more coffee, refusing to allow the emotion a foothold.

When he turned back again, he felt as if he'd regained his control.

"One thing is for certain," he said. "We need to stay vigilant until we know what's going on. One or the other of us needs to be with Kathryn at all times. We can't afford to leave her alone for a second."

Sherry nodded in agreement. "I'll make certain all the doors and windows are locked whenever you're not here, and she can take her naps on the floor in the living room."

"Tomorrow is my day off. Maybe I should see about getting some sort of security system installed." Anger swept through him at the very idea. How dare anyone attempt to breach the sanctity of his home...his family.

Before he could say anything more, the phone rang. He answered. "Boss...everything all right there?" Andy's voice boomed across the line. "Etta Mae said you tore out of here like the hounds of hell were chasing you."

"Somebody attempted a break-in through my bedroom window, but everything is fine," Clint replied.

"A break-in? You want me to come right over with the fingerprint kit?" Andy's voice rose in pitch, indicating the excitement of a normally bored deputy who suddenly had the prospect of a real crime to investigate.

"I've already boarded up the window," Clint said, knowing Andy would be disappointed. "But, if you want to come over and take a look around, maybe you can see something that I missed." With a hurried goodbye, Andy hung up. Clint did the same and turned back to Sherry.

"Andy is coming by to look over the scene," he explained.

"You think he'll find anything?" Sherry asked.

"Nah, but he was so excited I didn't have the heart to tell him that it's doubtful he'll find anything."

Sherry smiled at him, a full, generous smile that warmed him from head to toe. "You're a nice man, Clint Graham." Her eyes held a softness that tormented him...like lush green forests beckoning him inside.

"When I find who is responsible for all this, I won't be such a nice guy," he returned evenly. "I'm going outside to wait for Andy." He turned and left, needing to escape the small confines of the kitchen and Sherry's tempting green eyes.

Nearly two hours later Clint said goodbye to a disappointed Andy. Just as Clint had suspected, there had been no evidence for Andy to investigate.

Darkness was approaching fast. Night clouds raced across the sky to usurp the last glow of twilight. As Andy's car lights disappeared down the road, Clint leaned against the garage door.

Night. And Sherry would be slipping into the nightgown he'd accidently seen her wearing...the burgundy silky one with tiny spaghetti straps and the teasing low neckline. He felt his body's response as he envisioned her. His pulse quickened and his blood felt hot inside his veins.

Night. And Sherry would be sleeping in a bed beneath his roof, but not in his arms, not sharing the warmth of his bed.

He swiped a hand across his jaw thoughtfully. With one simple kiss his relationship with Sherry had suddenly become complicated and strained.

Hell, who was he fooling?

There had been nothing simple about the kiss they had shared. It had consumed him, had lit a fire in the pit of his stomach the likes of which he'd never known before.

It had been a big mistake. What bothered him more than anything was how badly he wanted to repeat the mistake.

Chapter Six

Clint was on the telephone when Sherry entered the kitchen the next morning. As she poured herself a cup of coffee, she tried not to notice how devastatingly handsome he looked.

His worn jeans fit him like a second skin, emphasizing his lean hips and taut buttocks. His short-sleeved pale-blue shirt displayed his biceps and complemented the darkness of his hair and the azure hue of his eyes.

She carried her cup to the table, where she whispered a good-morning greeting to Kathryn, who returned the greeting with a happy smile, then she left the kitchen so Clint could speak in privacy.

In the living room she stood at the front window and stared out into the brilliant morning sunshine.

She took a sip of her coffee, her thoughts drifting over the events of the day before.

It had been a day of roller-coaster emotions, first the fear and drama of the near break-in, then the joy and ensuing despair over the kiss she and Clint had shared.

She touched her lips, the memory of that kiss still lingering as if the imprint of his mouth had been burned forever into hers.

She'd thought she'd forgotten the utter pleasure of Clint's lips against hers. She'd believed she'd long ago forgotten how easily his kisses had been able to stoke a deep desire inside her.

However, the moment his lips had touched hers, it had been like coming home after a long absence.

"Don't fool yourself," she whispered softly as she turned away from the window and sat down heavily on the sofa.

Clint's kiss might have had the warmth of a homecoming welcome, but Sherry couldn't forget that she could never be the woman Clint deserved. The homecoming, at best, would be temporary.

The evening before had been tense. She and Clint had watched television for a couple of hours, allowing the mundane sitcoms to take the place of any real conversation.

Sherry had sat on the floor next to Kathryn, while Clint sat on the sofa. Yet, even with the adequate physical distance between them, Sherry couldn't mentally distance herself enough for comfort.

The kiss had altered things, destroyed the easy camaraderie they normally enjoyed. She was far too aware of him on a physical level, far too aware of her own want where he was concerned.

For the first time in her life she cursed her virginity, wished she could be the kind of woman who could separate heart and body. She wished she could just fall into bed with him, with no regrets the morning after. But she couldn't.

When she finally gave herself completely and wholly to a man physically, she knew she would give her heart, as well. She wanted it to be a forever kind of giving, not just a temporary pleasure.

When the news had come on, Sherry had listened to the lead stories, one about a drug kingpin on trial in Kansas City, the second lead story about severe weather in western Kansas.

After those two stories had played, she'd excused herself and gone to bed. To her surprise she'd slept deeply, without interruption, without dreams.

She'd awakened refreshed, feeling as if she could face being with Clint for another day and not do anything foolish.

She heard him hang up, then a moment later he came into the living room carrying Kathryn. ''How would you like to take a drive with us?''

She looked at him in surprise. ''Where?''

He sat on the sofa next to her, Kathryn on his lap.

''That was Stan on the phone. He got me

Candy's new address. She still lives in Kansas City." He held up a piece of paper where he'd written the address. "I thought we'd take a little ride, see what she has to say."

"When do you want to go?" she asked.

"Right now. The sooner the better."

"Shouldn't you try to call her first?" Sherry asked.

Clint shook his head. "She should be home on a Saturday and I don't want to give her any warning, and I don't want to confront her over the phone. I want to do this in person." He smiled at her. "If we leave now we can stop on the way and get breakfast. I figure breakfast out has got to be as good as the breakfasts you make."

"I've never made you breakfast," Sherry protested.

"Exactly," he said with an easy laugh.

Sherry returned his laughter, grateful that somehow the morning had brought with it the easy friendship they normally shared. Apparently he'd forgotten about the kiss, and she intended to do the same. "Okay. I'm game." She stood. "Just let me get my purse and check the diaper bag to make sure we have everything Kathryn might need."

"While you do that, I'll go get the car seat secured," Clint replied. "We'll be waiting in the car."

Sherry grabbed her purse from her bedroom, pausing for a moment to check her reflection in the mirror. She ran a brush through her short, blond-streaked hair, then pulled from her purse a tube of lipstick.

"What are you doing?" she asked the woman in the mirror, lipstick poised in ready position.

Why was she putting on lipstick? To give her lips a dewy, kissable sheen? For whom?

Kissing Clint had been a mistake the day before, one she didn't intend to repeat. She was going to forget all about it. With renewed resolution she put the lipstick back in her purse without using it, then turned away from the mirror and hurried out of the room.

A few minutes later she slid into the passenger side of Clint's car. Clint was behind the wheel, and Kathryn was safely secured in her car seat in the back.

"All set?" he asked.

She nodded and he backed out of the driveway. By the time they reached the highway leading toward Kansas City, the movement of the car had lulled Kathryn to sleep.

Initially Clint seemed tense, and his gaze darted often to the rearview mirror. Sherry realized he was keeping an eye out to make sure they weren't being followed, to make sure another kidnapping attempt wasn't imminent.

"Everything all right?" she asked worriedly as he changed lanes for the fourth time.

"Fine. Just being cautious."

He switched lanes several more times, his gaze constantly darting to the mirror, then after about twenty minutes of driving, he visibly relaxed.

Sherry did the same, settling against the seat and watching the scenery fly by. "There's nothing prettier than spring in the midwest," she observed.

"Unless it's autumn," Clint replied.

"You're right, autumn is nice, too," she agreed. "I love the crisp air and the scent of burning leaves."

"And cool nights made just for snuggling," Clint added. His gaze caught hers for a moment, then he jerked his attention back to the road. "Yeah, autumn is pretty nice."

Sherry could imagine snuggling with Clint beneath the heavy, navy bedspread on his bed, the warmth of his body keeping the chill of the night away.

She cleared her throat and consciously shoved such thoughts away. "This is off the subject, but last night while you were outside with Andy, I called Walt and gave him my resignation."

Clint jerked his head to stare at her in surprise. "You're kidding! What are you going to do? Go back to teaching?"

"I don't know...maybe. To be honest, I'm not sure what I want to do. I just realized it was time for a change." She stared out the window thoughtfully.

In the three days with Kathryn, the little girl had

taught Sherry a valuable lesson—that she could spend time with children, love children and not feel the torturous ache of her own infertility. "I've got a little money saved up. I can afford to take some time and decide exactly what I want to do."

Clint flashed her a smile and reached out to lightly touch her hand. "I'm glad, Sherry. I never understood what made you quit teaching and go to work for Walt in the first place."

She nodded, then gazed out the window once more. No, he'd never understood. Nobody had understood the depth of her pain when she'd discovered she couldn't have children.

Her mother had cried with her, then in her own pragmatic way had told Sherry to get over it and move on with her life. Sherry's sister had dealt with the issue by studiously avoiding any and all talk of children.

And Clint had said all the right words—that it didn't matter, that he loved her anyway. But she'd seen the momentary flare of disappointment in his eyes and she couldn't get past it.

She hadn't broken off her engagement to him immediately upon learning she'd never have children. She'd waited a month, an agonizing month, then had told him her feelings for him had changed, that she didn't love him anymore.

She hadn't wanted his pity, hadn't wanted him to know that it had been her barrenness that had destroyed their plans. It had been easier to pretend she'd made a mistake about loving him.

"You've suddenly fallen terribly quiet," Clint said, breaking into her thoughts.

She shrugged. "Just thinking."

"About?"

She smiled at him. "Nothing important."

He eased down his window a little, allowing in the fresh, fragrant spring air. "You know, this time of year always reminds me of when we first met. It was on a day just like this."

Her smile deepened. "You were the new, handsome deputy in town and I had just finished college."

"I wasn't at all sure I was going to be able to adjust to a little town like Armordale after living in Kansas City, but the minute I saw you I knew I'd adjust fine." He cast her another grin, one of warm friendship and teasing humor. "You were so sassy and full of energy."

"And you were so full of yourself, strutting around in your uniform and eyeing everyone with that authoritative glare."

"I did not strut," Clint laughed in protest.

"Yes, you did," she returned with a teasing grin. "You had that big-city strut that had every female in town half-crazy about you, and every male in town ready to punch you out."

"Now that you bring it up, I did seem to have a lot of men swinging at my face that first year." He frowned somberly. "I'll admit I probably seemed a little arrogant, but it was really defensiveness."

"Defensiveness? What were you defensive about?" She eyed him curiously. The idea that Clint would ever be insecure or vulnerable seemed alien. From the moment she'd met him, he'd always seemed in control, confident in himself and his abilities.

"I was only twenty-three, fresh out of the academy, when Sheriff Bodine hired me.

"He had misgivings about me because of my youth and inexperience. It was really important to me to prove that I could handle the job, not only to everyone in Armordale, but especially to myself."

"Your parents died before you graduated from the police academy, didn't they?" she asked softly. In all the years they had known each other, Clint had never said much about his parents, only telling Sherry that they'd died in a car accident just before he'd moved to Armordale.

"Yeah, they died a month before graduation."

She noticed that his hands tightened on the steering wheel and his features were closed, forbidding her to delve further into the topic of his parents.

She wondered if Clint's reticence to discuss his parents was because of his grief over their death, or because the relationship between parents and son had been strained. All she knew was that he almost never mentioned them.

"You ready for breakfast?" he asked as he pointed to a truck stop ahead.

"Sure, sounds great," she agreed.

Within minutes Clint and Sherry were seated opposite each other at a booth and Kathryn was happily banging a spoon on her high-chair tray.

"I can't believe what a good-natured baby she is," Sherry marveled. Kathryn had awakened as they'd carried her into the restaurant, an instant smile lighting her cherub features.

"She takes after her daddy," Clint replied, winking at the little girl.

Sherry wondered what Clint would do if they discovered the baby wasn't Candy's and consequently not his. She had a feeling his heart would break. He'd embraced Kathryn as his own so completely and he seemed to have pushed any doubts about her paternity away.

The waitress appeared at their table, an older woman whose name tag read Alma. She handed them each a menu, then aahed and oohed over Kathryn.

"It's hard to tell who she looks most like," Alma said. "She's definitely got her daddy's eyes, but I think she maybe has her mama's nose. She sure is a doll baby."

"Thanks," Clint said before Sherry could explain that she wasn't Kathryn's mother. They ordered, and the waitress disappeared back into the kitchen.

"I guess we look like a respectable family enjoying breakfast out," he said. "Funny how people are willing to believe illusions."

A respectable family—a loving, family unit. Just an illusion, Sherry had to remind herself again and again as they enjoyed the meal. They took turns feeding Kathryn from their plates, cheering as she accepted what they offered and laughing as she spit out what she didn't like.

It could have been like this, Sherry thought with a touch of bitterness. It should have been like this. She and Clint should be married, with a child of their own. It was what she'd dreamed about, what she'd longed for…and it was what cruel fate had stolen from her.

She tried to dispel her negative thoughts. She'd made a conscious decision five years ago to allow Clint the freedom to have all the dreams she'd once held for herself.

There was no going back for them…and no going forward. She would never have children of her own, and after seeing Clint with Kathryn, she would never ask him to sacrifice the joy of true fatherhood.

No, she and Clint would never share a life, but that didn't mean there weren't other options for her. An idea swirled around in the back of her head, a nebulous whisper of hope.

They finished the meal but lingered over coffee, as if reluctant to continue their journey. They were both extremely aware that the trip might end in Kathryn being reunited with her mother.

Their conversation ranged from Walt and Betty's running feud over Rover the flower-eating dog, to Andy's futile crush on Ramona Baker, the young woman who had recently bought the florist shop in town.

When a silence fell between them, Sherry spoke aloud the thought that had been flitting through her head. "When all this with Kathryn is settled, I think I'm going to check into adopting a child. From what I understand, they're allowing single people to do that now."

Clint frowned and signaled the waitress for their check. "You know I've never been a big believer in adoption," he said. "I'd rather have no children than adopt any. But you have to do what's best for you."

He'd closed off, pulled the shades over his eyes and locked the door on his emotions. Just as he'd done years ago when they'd had a theoretical discussion about the merits of adoption.

The discussion had taken place before Sherry had known she'd never have children. She'd told Clint she'd like to have two children and adopt two, and it had been then that Clint had told her he'd never consider adoption.

Clint went to the register to pay for the meal as Sherry washed Kathryn's face and hands with a damp napkin. When she was finished, she gazed at

Clint and in that moment she realized why she'd brought up the adoption issue.

It had been a last attempt to see if there was any hope for a future between them. As she picked up the little girl, a strange ache throbbed in her chest— an ache she thought she'd long ago resolved.

She loved Clint. The emotion tore through her with unexpected clarity. She'd never, ever stopped loving him. Despite her wanting the contrary, he'd been in her heart all these years.

As she hugged Kathryn close, she recognized the strange ache for what it was, and she was surprised that after all this time she could still hurt. It was the confirmation that she and Clint could never, would never share their lives.

Chapter Seven

As they drew closer to Kansas City, Clint's nerves jangled and jumped in the pit of his stomach, making him sorry he'd indulged himself in a huge breakfast.

Sherry had been silent since they'd left the truck stop, as if something important occupied her thoughts.

Her floral scent filled the car and eddied in his head. He thought about the sparkle in her eyes, her laughter and animation as they'd shared their meals with Kathryn.

It was a shame she'd never have children of her own. She would have made a wonderful mother. She had the gift of laughter and a deep well of love to share—but not with me, he reminded himself.

Her announcement that she intended to adopt a

child had been a necessary slap to his senses, reminding him that on the issue of children and family, he and Sherry were worlds apart.

She knew how he felt about adoption. It had been the subject of the one heated argument they'd ever had. She knew how he felt, and her decision to adopt on her own merely served to remind him that she didn't want him in her life on a permanent basis.

She loved him as a friend, and that was all. He frowned and tightened his grip on the steering wheel. But did a friend offer another friend such heat, such intense hunger in a kiss?

He shot her a surreptitious gaze. The late-morning sunlight drifted in the window to stroke shiny highlights into her hair. Clint's fingers tingled as he remembered how her hair had felt...silky soft and invitingly touchable.

Wearing a pair of jeans and a pullover red-and-white-striped top, she should have looked casually relaxed, but she didn't. Tension tugged at her features, and when her gaze turned and caught his, he saw a mournful sadness in her eyes.

"You okay?" he asked.

She nodded. "I guess I ate too much." She flashed him a quicksilver smile, but the gesture lacked life. She stared back out the front window. "I think I've got a little stomachache."

"A stomachache...or a heartache?" he asked.

Her gaze jerked back to him sharply. "A heartache? Why would you think I have a heartache?'' Her voice held a defensive edge.

He shrugged and snapped the blinker on to indicate he was taking the next exit. ''I know it's only been a couple of days, but I've seen how much Kathryn has managed to capture your heart. I'm sure it hurts to realize it's very possible we're delivering her back to her mother.''

Sherry visibly relaxed and turned her head to gaze at the little girl happily babbling in the back seat. She turned back around and released a deep sigh. ''Yes, she has managed to capture my heart, just as she has yours.''

Clint nodded. ''She's done more than capture my heart,'' he replied softly. ''She's become the keeper of my dreams, and these are dreams I didn't even know I possessed.''

The awe that had been with him since the moment he recognized the possibility that the little girl was his filled him so completely, it made any further speech impossible.

Sherry reached over and touched his shoulder. ''If you really are her father, she's the luckiest little girl alive.''

If. A word that held all things possible and all things impossible. He didn't even want to consider the possibility that Kathryn wasn't his.

Because Sherry would never have children of her own, she'd never experience the depth of love Clint felt for Kathryn. That broke his heart on Sherry's behalf. Adopting a child wouldn't be the same, could never be the same as having one who carried your genes, who came from your very soul.

"If Candy really is her mother, then I'm going to have a long hard talk with her before I just hand Kathryn back to her," Clint said, more to himself than to Sherry. "I have to make sure she never pulls anything like this again." Reaching into his pocket, he pulled out the slip of paper that contained Candy's address. "This apartment building should be just up ahead," he said to Sherry. "There are several apartment buildings in this block, so we'll have to watch for the actual address." He slowed the car to a near creep.

"There." Sherry pointed to a six-story brick building on the left side of the road.

Clint pulled into an empty parking space across the street and shut off the engine. For a moment he simply sat and stared at the apartment building where Stan had said Candy now lived.

In the next few minutes his life would be forever changed. He'd learn if Kathryn was really his or not. In an instant his mind exploded with visions of weekend visits, of trips to the park and sticky kisses, of ballet lessons and frilly dresses.

Drawing a deep breath, he opened his car door and got out. Sherry did the same. As Sherry grabbed the diaper bag, Clint unbuckled Kathryn and drew her into his arms.

She laughed and reached for the end of his nose.

Clint dodged her grasp and instead hugged her tight against him. She smelled of baby powder and innocence, and a tide of protective love welled up inside him.

"Let's get this over with," he said to Sherry, who nodded and fell into step with him. Together they entered the apartment building and went to the bank of elevators. "I'm hoping since it's Saturday morning, Candy will be home."

"What floor?" Sherry asked as they stepped into the elevator.

"Sixth," Clint said. "According to Stan, Candy lives in 603."

Sherry punched the button for the sixth floor. They rode up in silence. Even Kathryn was somber and quiet, as if sensing something amiss.

When the elevator reached the sixth floor, the doors dinged open and they stepped out. Right in front of them was apartment 603.

Clint didn't hesitate. Now that he stood before the door that would give him the answers he sought, he was eager to get it over and done with. He knocked loudly on the door, then looked at Sherry.

She stood clutching the diaper bag to her chest. She returned his gaze, and in her eyes he saw the abiding friendship and deep support he'd come to count on through the years.

He also saw the pain of a woman who'd grown to love a child and now might have to relinquish the bond that had grown between them.

He realized that for the past several days, both he and Sherry had been living a fantasy...sharing the joys of parenthood. He also realized that giving up Kathryn would be almost as difficult on her as it was on him.

He knocked once again on the door, then reached for Sherry's hand, wanting to support her and needing the warmth of the physical connection for himself.

"Hold your horses," a familiar female voice called out from behind the door. There was a jangle of a chain lock being removed, then the door opened.

Candy looked just as Clint remembered her. Platinum-blond hair was perfectly coiffed and her eye makeup was dramatic and bold, emphasizing cold, blue eyes.

"Clint!" She looked at him in surprise. "What are you doing here?" She turned and looked at Sherry. "And Shirley, isn't it?"

"Sherry," Sherry corrected dryly. She pulled her hand from Clint's and took a step backward, as if not wanting to get too close to the woman she'd described as a man-eater.

"Ah, yes...Sherry. What's going on?" Candy looked from one to the other, her obvious confusion appearing genuine. "Cute baby," she observed. "Is she yours?" she asked Sherry.

Clint felt as if a bullet had been shot through his

heart. "Actually, we thought she might be yours," he said.

Candy's eyes widened. "Mine?" Candy's hands fluttered in the air, her nails long, and painted a vivid red that matched her lipstick. "Good God, why would you think something like that?"

"She was left on my doorstep several days ago with a note that implied I was her father." Clint's voice sounded dull and lifeless to his own ears. That's how he felt—lifeless, dead inside. "Her, uh, conception would have occurred about the time I was seeing you...so I thought maybe—"

"Oh, please," Candy said with amusement. "Perish the very thought. I don't find children particularly cute or amusing, and the last thing I'd do would be to have one of my own." She grinned at Clint. "You'd better check your black book again, darling...see who else you might have been seeing besides me."

Clint believed her. Candy was the last woman on earth who would choose to have a child. A child required love and nurturing, and Candy was too busy loving and nurturing herself to attend to any baby.

"Sorry to bother you," he said. He turned and punched the elevator button.

"Clint?"

He turned back to face the attractive woman. "You're looking real good," she cooed. "If you ever want a second go-round, just give me a call."

"Thanks, Candy, but I think I'll pass," he returned. "One round with you was more than enough for me."

Candy's eyes narrowed, and without another word she slammed her apartment door.

"I can't believe I actually dated that woman," Clint said as he and Sherry stepped into the elevator. "Why didn't you check me into a mental institution when I started seeing her? I must have been crazy." He carefully kept his thoughts distant from the fact that the baby in his arms was no longer his daughter, but rather an abandoned baby, a stranger.

"You're a big boy and nobody was holding a gun to your head," she replied.

They spoke no more as they left the apartment building and got back into the car. Clint secured Kathryn in her car seat, his heart aching with renewed pain.

Not his. The baby that had captured his heart, been embraced by his very soul, wasn't really his. There would be no weekend visits, no trips to the zoo or ballet lessons. There would be no sticky kisses and Father's Day surprises where he and little Kathryn were concerned.

As he started the car engine, he glanced over at Sherry. Somehow he knew his loss would have been easier to bear if Sherry loved him. If he held Sherry's heart, then the empty place inside him wouldn't be quite so empty.

As it was, the emptiness rang deep and painful, and he'd never in his life felt so utterly alone.

Clint was silent on the drive home. Several times Sherry tried to think of words to say, words of comfort and support, but each time she turned to look at him, the misery on his face kept her silent.

In many ways Clint had always been a private man. Although generous in nature, Sherry had learned a long time ago that he kept his emotions under a tight wrap, sharing little of the feelings that were inside him.

A year ago, when Clint's best friend in Armordale died in a tragic car accident, Sherry had gone to the funeral with Clint. She'd seen the grief that played on his features, felt the sorrow that radiated from him, but he'd refused to speak of his feelings and hadn't sought any comfort from her.

It was the same way now. She sensed that he'd shut down, closed off, but she ached with her own need to comfort him.

How horrible it must be, she thought, to truly believe you had a child, to allow that child into your hopes and dreams, into your heart and soul, only to discover the child wasn't yours after all.

Somehow his pain was even worse than hers. Once she'd learned she couldn't have children, there had been no hope to tease her, no possibility of dreams coming true to torment her.

She waited until they were almost back to Armordale before she finally broke the silence. "So, what do we do now…about Kathryn?"

"I suppose Monday I'll have to contact Social Services," he said. She heard the deep reluctance in his voice.

"Don't you dare," Sherry replied. "There's no way I'll let you do that."

He cast her a sideways glance. "But you told me you'd only help me out for three days."

"Well, I lied," she replied succinctly. Then she reached over and placed a hand on his shoulder. "Clint, just because we've found out she isn't yours doesn't mean we just throw her to the system." She dropped her hand.

"And I don't want to throw her to the system," he said after a moment of hesitation. "But how long can we keep this arrangement going? How long are you willing to put your own life on hold?"

"As long as it takes," she replied. She turned around to look at the little girl sleeping in the car seat. "As long as she needs me."

She shifted position and once again looked at him. "Besides, in the note the mother said she would be back for her in a week or so. That's only a couple more days away." Sherry offered Clint a teasing smile. "Surely you can survive having me as a house guest for a little while longer."

No responding light of humor lit his eyes, and he made no reply.

Sherry fell silent once again, her heart aching

with the hurt that he must be feeling. At least he had the consolation that although Kathryn wasn't his, he could still have his own children.

She had a feeling that Kathryn had opened his heart and because of his temporary fatherhood he'd be more eager than ever to get married and start a family of his own.

Again pain soared through her—this time not a reflection of his pain, but rather her own. It was the deep anguish of her love for him, a love that forever would remain locked in her heart where it couldn't flourish, would never be shared.

She knew she would probably live the rest of her life loving Clint. And he would end up spending the rest of his life with some lucky woman, making babies and fulfilling his dreams without her.

Tears burned in her eyes, and she averted her gaze out the passenger window and sneaked a hand up to swipe them away. She'd meant what she said. She would remain in his house for as long as Kathryn needed her.

But when Kathryn's mother came to get her, when Kathryn was no longer a part of their lives, Sherry knew one of the changes she would have to make in her life was to see less of Clint. With her love for him so strong, so alive inside her, she knew she had to make a difficult resolution. She had to let go of their friendship, because she knew she couldn't stand to remain his friend and know she'd never, ever be his future.

"I have a confession to make," Clint said as he pulled into his driveway.

Sherry swallowed the last of her tears and looked at him in surprise. "What kind of a confession?" she asked.

"I haven't really aggressively pursued finding out who Kathryn is. I was so certain that she was Candy's I haven't expended much energy seeking any other answers." He shut off the engine and raked a hand through his hair.

"So what do you have in mind?"

"Maybe I need to check with the hospital here in town, see what babies were born five to seven months ago and who the parents are. It makes sense that Kathryn's mother lives right here in Armordale."

"Why does that make sense?" Sherry asked.

"The mother apparently knew I was the sheriff. It's obvious she left Kathryn here because she thought I could protect her from whoever is after her." He frowned thoughtfully. "It's possible what we're dealing with here is a custody issue. Maybe it was Kathryn's father who tried to break into the house and snatch her."

"That makes sense," Sherry agreed. Somehow it seemed less horrific to think that it was somebody who loved Kathryn who might have tried to take her.

"I think I'll spend the afternoon making some calls, see what I can find out," Clint said. He got out of the car, then opened the back door and un-buckled the car seat. Kathryn woke up, and in-stantly her face was wreathed in a toothless, happy grin.

Sherry saw the spasm of pain that tightened Clint's features. She followed them inside the house, wondering how on earth either of them would survive loving Kathryn, then losing her.

The afternoon was somber. Clint spent the rest of the day on the phone while Sherry tried to soothe an unusually fussy Kathryn.

It was as if the little girl sensed the gloom that had overtaken the atmosphere in the house and had picked up on the sadness of her two caretakers.

Sherry tried to give her a bottle, then attempted to rock her to sleep. She walked with her, sang to her, but nothing seemed to soothe her.

Finally Sherry sat down on the living room floor and tried to play with Kathryn, but Kathryn was having nothing to do with it. She pushed away the toys Sherry offered, her lower lip quivering with the threat of tears.

Sherry looked up as Clint came into the room, a piece of paper in hand. "Well, I talked to the hospital and got the names of all the women who had children in or around the right time period." He sat down at the sofa, then frowned as Kathryn screwed up her face and started to cry in earnest. "What's wrong with her?"

"I don't know," Sherry admitted. She stood,

then leaned down and picked up the crying baby girl. "I can't seem to do anything to make her happy."

Appearing reluctant, Clint held out his arms. "Let me try," he said. Kathryn went willingly into his arms and snuggled against his broad chest as if that was where she belonged. With a sigh of resignation, Clint patted her little bottom and when he looked at Sherry, his dark-blue eyes radiated anguish.

"I really believed she was mine," he said, his voice husky with suppressed emotion.

Sherry sat down next to him. "I know." She stroked a finger down his strong jawline, wishing there was some way she could ease his pain, so similar to the one she'd lived with for the past five years.

He put his arm around her and drew her against his side. There was nothing even vaguely threatening about his embrace, no hint of the fire and desire that had flamed between them when they'd kissed. They were two friends, silently sharing emotions, silently offering comfort.

Kathryn slept against his chest, each slumbering breath puffing out her chubby cheeks. Sherry closed her eyes and existed only for the moment, with his warmth and familiar scent surrounding her.

She didn't want to think about what would never be, didn't want to contemplate the fact that when everything was resolved with Kathryn, she intended to get on with her life, without Clint's friendship to sustain her.

She lost track of time, thought perhaps she might have fallen asleep, safe in the shelter of his arms. "Want to take another ride with me?" His deep voice pulled her from her drowsy state.

"Where?" she asked. She sat up, the side of her body cooling with the absence of his.

"Check out the people on this list, make sure they all have their babies with them."

"Okay," she agreed. She had the feeling that now he'd discovered Kathryn wasn't his child, the reluctance he'd felt before in searching for her parents was gone.

It didn't take them long to load back into the car. Sherry read the first name on the list aloud. "Betty Miller."

"Cross her off," Clint instructed. "I just saw her and her husband pushing their baby down Main day before yesterday."

Sherry dutifully crossed a line through the name. "Rita Clemmons. Isn't that Pastor Clemmons's wife?"

"Yeah, I think so."

Sherry frowned. "Surely they wouldn't abandon their baby on your doorstep."

"Maybe not. But we aren't leaving any stones unturned. We'll swing by their house and make sure their little girl is still in their custody."

All trace of any former emotion was gone from

him. It was as if he'd successfully removed himself from all feeling. A wave of envy swept through Sherry. How she wished she could do the same— not only remove herself from the heartache of loving Kathryn, but from the bigger anguish of loving Clint.

The answer to whether the Clemmonses had their baby with them or not was answered easily. When they drove by the tidy home, the family was in the front yard. Rita Clemmons held her daughter while Pastor Clemmons worked in a flowerbed.

Sherry and Clint waved to the couple as they drove by, then Sherry looked at the last and final name on the list. "Molly Ketchum." Sherry frowned. "I don't think I know her."

"She's only eighteen and was the only unmarried person to have a baby in that particular time frame. She lives with her parents over on Oak Street."

"How do you know all that?" Sherry asked.

He grinned. "When I called the hospital, I spoke to Tracy Witfield."

Sherry laughed and held up a hand. "No further explanation is necessary." Tracy Witfield was Armordale's biggest gossip. Somehow she managed to know all the business of every person in the small town, whether it was public or private.

"Apparently, you living in my house the past couple of days has generated a bit of gossip," he added.

Sherry groaned inwardly. She hadn't thought of what everyone must be saying.

"Tracy told me that Fred is running a pool down at his barber shop. Whoever guesses the exact date we get married wins a lifetime of free haircuts."

"Well, that's one pool Fred won't have to worry about paying out," she replied lightly, and tried to ignore the heart pang her words evoked.

"Yeah...I guess so."

He didn't look at her, but she thought she'd heard regret in his voice. Regret about what? That they weren't really ever going to get married? Clint didn't love her, not really. He hadn't even tried to kiss her again after the kiss they had shared the day of the break-in.

She wondered if he'd ever really loved her as she wanted, needed to be loved. After all, it had always been Clint who had managed to call a halt to their kisses and caresses. It had always been Clint who had maintained control and stopped any real lovemaking before it really began. He'd known how important it was for her to be a virgin on her wedding night.

Maybe he'd never really loved her as desperately, as passionately as she'd loved him. Again she told herself how necessary it was that when this was all over, she leave him behind.

Their friendship had become a crutch, making it easy for her not to get on with her life. The friendship and companionship had eased her loneliness

and filled empty hours. She hadn't needed to date
or find a boyfriend while she had Clint in her life.

Kathryn had somehow managed to open her
heart, melt away the icy barrier she'd erected long
ago, and what Sherry was left with was a heart that
loved Clint. But she knew it was finally time to
move on.

They arrived at the Ketchums', and Clint explained the situation to Molly's mother. The older
woman called to Molly, and the eighteen-year-old
mother came out of her bedroom carrying a dark-
haired, dark-eyed little girl about Kathryn's age.

Clint thanked them for their time, then he, Sherry
and Kathryn once again were in the car heading
back home.

"So what do we do now?" Sherry asked.

Clint shrugged. "I guess we just keep Kathryn
safe and wait to see what happens next."

During the next couple of days they once again
fell into a routine of sorts. Clint went to work each
morning while Sherry took care of Kathryn, then in
the evenings they shared the responsibility of the
little girl.

It was much the way it had been before they'd
gone to see Candy, but with some change. Sherry
tried to maintain as much emotional and physical
distance between herself and Clint as possible.

And she watched as Clint tried futilely to distance himself from the little girl who'd captured his

heart. He would come home from work and she'd fuss until he picked her up and played with her.

Sherry had never loved him as much as when he was rocking Kathryn or making silly faces just to hear her giggle. The love that rocked through her only managed to reconfirm her decision to eventually cut him completely out of her life.

As soon as Kathryn was back with her family, Sherry would start being unavailable to Clint. She'd be busy when he invited her over for pizza, have something else to do when he wanted her to meet him for lunch. Eventually he'd stop calling, stop asking her to do things with him. Eventually they would just become nodding acquaintances who had once shared a past.

But even knowing this didn't stop the fluttering of her stomach each time she looked at him. If only he wasn't so darned handsome, if only those deep-blue eyes of his, the strength of his jawline, his soft, smiling lips didn't stir her so. If only his shoulders weren't so broad, his hips so lean. If only he didn't cause her head to spin and her body to tingle each and every time she looked at him.

She'd been angry with him when he'd first asked for her help, afraid that she wouldn't be able to stand the grief of caring for a child, loving a child and knowing she'd never belong to her. Sherry hadn't considered the real torture would be caring about Clint, loving him and knowing he would never belong to her.

It was early evening on Wednesday, and as usual they were all in the living room. Clint had brought home from work a package of large, stuffed blocks, and he sat in the middle of the floor, building a tower of the blocks for Kathryn's delight.

Kathryn eyed him with watchful eyes, not attempting to join in the process but waiting... waiting. And when the tower tumbled to the floor, her giggles filled the room, mingling with the deep, robust laughter of Clint.

Sherry wondered if it were possible for her to love Clint any deeper. She thought not. Her love for him transcended anything she'd ever before experienced. Her love for him knew no boundaries or conditions. It was just there...inside her, filling her up with both joy and aching sorrow.

It was easy for Sherry to imagine a lifetime of nights just like this one, watching Clint and Kathryn together; nights of tucking her in and singing her lullabies; nights of Clint and her going to bed together, renewing their passion and love for each other.

Maybe Kathryn's mother will never come back for her, she thought. Then Clint and I can keep her, raise her as our own, share not only in her life but in each other's lives.

It was a stupid fantasy. If Kathryn's mother didn't eventually turn up, then Clint would turn her over to Social Services. He had told her he'd never consider adopting a child, so he wouldn't want to keep and raise Kathryn, which in effect would be the same as an adoption.

She'd never understood his views on the adoption process and had never been able to make him explain in depth the reason for his adamant negative feelings. He'd made it clear to her that he didn't approve, but had never gone into the reasons why he felt that way.

Still, the adoption issue alone spoke volumes about why they could never, would never be together as a romantic couple.

It was just a little after eight when Sherry fed Kathryn some cereal and gave her a bottle. When she finished, Clint took the drowsy child from her. "I'll put her to bed," he said.

Sherry nodded, knowing that meant Clint would spend the remainder of the evening in his room. They were still sticking to the rule that Kathryn didn't remain anywhere alone. Neither of them had forgotten that somewhere, somebody seemed to want the little girl.

As Kathryn and Clint disappeared into his bedroom, Sherry settled back on the sofa and turned on the television. She'd watch a little TV until she got tired enough to sleep, tired enough not to dream of Clint.

She had just gotten interested in a medical drama series when the doorbell rang. Sherry jumped up off the sofa, wanting to hurry to answer before whoever it was awakened Kathryn.

She opened the door to find a petite, youthful blond woman. Vivid-blue eyes widened as the woman stared at Sherry. "Who...who are you?" she asked. "Where is Dave?"

"There's no Dave here. You must have the wrong address."

"It's not the wrong address." Tears filled her eyes. "Oh, my God, what's happened? Where's Kathryn? Where's my baby girl? Oh, dear God, what have you done with her?"

Chapter Eight

Clint heard the doorbell and opened his bedroom door to listen as Sherry answered. The moment he heard the woman at the door say Kathryn's name, he knew who she was and why she was here.

He looked at the little girl, who slept peacefully in her crib. What he didn't intend to do was simply hand Kathryn over without some sort of explanation from the woman who had left her behind. Kathryn's mother had abandoned her baby, and he'd have a damned good reason from her or she wouldn't get Kathryn back easily. That sweet little baby girl deserved nothing less.

He left the bedroom, leaving Kathryn sleeping in the crib, relatively certain she would be safe. The window was still boarded over, making it impossible for anyone to get into the room.

"We have your daughter," Sherry explained to the weeping woman. "She's in the other room."

"Oh, thank God. Is she all right?" The woman grabbed the sleeve of Sherry's pale-blue blouse. "Please get her for me," the woman exclaimed.

"Sherry, I'll handle this," Clint said.

He opened the front door wide enough for the woman to enter the living room. "Have a seat," he said, and pointed to the sofa.

"I don't want to sit down. I just want my daughter." The woman swiped at her eyes, a glint of impatient anger shining through the tears. "I don't know what's going on, what you've done with Dave, but I want my daughter back right now."

"You are in no position to make demands. Now, sit down," Clint thundered.

To his surprise, both Sherry and the woman sat on either end of the sofa. For a long moment he stared at Kathryn's mother.

She was small and thin, with huge blue eyes and light-blond, shoulder-length hair. She looked young, and he noted that she wore no wedding ring.

He walked over to the small table just inside the front door, picked up his badge, then tossed it on the coffee table in front of her. "I'm Clint Graham, Sheriff of Armordale. I'll tell you right now, lady, unless you have some good answers, that baby isn't going anywhere with you. Now, let's start with your name."

"Mandy...Amanda Jenkins." She looked at

Sherry, then back to Clint. Once again her eyes filled with tears. She wrapped her arms around herself as if in an attempt to soothe an ache inside her. "I'm from Kansas City."

A sob escaped her, and she opened her arms, as if to show how empty they were. "Please...could I just see her...just hold her. This last week without her has felt like an entire lifetime."

Before Clint could reply, Sherry stood. "I'll be right back," she said, then disappeared down the hallway. Clint knew she was going to get Kathryn, and if she hadn't, he would have. Mandy's aching need was visible, tangible in the room.

It took several minutes before Sherry returned, hugging the sleeping Kathryn against her heart. Sherry's eyes were huge and glassy with the threat of tears.

Clint knew how difficult this was for her, and he cursed himself for ever getting her involved in the first place. The last thing he'd ever wanted to do was cause Sherry pain.

"Oh...oh," Mandy said, obviously speechless as Sherry gently transferred the baby to her. She clutched Kathryn against her, rubbing her hand across her head, down her little back. Tears once again fell from her eyes as she hugged Kathryn close as if afraid Clint and Sherry might try to take her away.

"Now, explain to me, who is this Dave you keep asking about?" Clint asked after he'd given her several moments to revel in her daughter's return. Sherry sat back down on the sofa, her features reflecting the haunting of a woman who had just lost something precious.

"David Freeman. He lived here for a while. He's Kathryn's father." She looked down at the sleeping child in her arms. "We stopped seeing each other soon after I discovered I was pregnant." A touch of bitterness darkened the blue of her eyes. "He wasn't interested in being a husband, and he definitely wasn't interested in being a daddy."

"I don't understand. Then why did you leave the baby here, on what you thought was his doorstep?" Sherry asked.

Again Mandy's eyes darkened. "Because I didn't know what else to do."

She rocked back and forth, as if comforting the sleeping baby, but Clint suspected she was soothing herself.

"I needed her to be someplace where I knew she'd be safe, where they wouldn't find her," she continued. "Since I hadn't seen Dave for a long time and I didn't list him on the birth certificate, I thought she'd be safe with him."

"Safe from what?" Clint asked. "From who?" He sat in the chair opposite the sofa.

She stopped rocking and released a heavy sigh. "It all started when I got called for jury duty in Kansas City—that's where I live. I'd had lots of friends serve on juries before and it didn't seem like a big deal. I thought it might be interesting, but I had no idea it would be life threatening.''

"Life threatening?'' Sherry eyed her curiously. "What kind of trial was it?''

"I was on the jury that just an hour or so ago convicted Maxwell Boothe,'' she said.

"Yeah, I read about that trial. Isn't he some kind of drug kingpin?'' Clint asked. Each evening the news had carried an update on the trial of the powerful, wealthy man who had been indicted several times before but never convicted.

Mandy nodded. "He's the top man in a drug cartel, he's a murderer and a blackmailer.'' She raised her chin a notch, pride gleaming from her eyes. "We convicted him, and he's going to be in prison for a very long time.''

"I don't understand. What does this have to do with Kathryn's safety?'' Sherry asked.

Mandy's arms tightened around Kathryn, and she leaned down and dropped a feathery kiss to her forehead. She drew a deep breath, her gaze shifting from Sherry to Clint, then back again. "The jury was seated late in the day. The judge dismissed us, told us to go home and make whatever preparations we needed to and to pack a bag because when we returned the next morning we would be sequestered.''

Sequestered. That was why she hadn't been able to care for Kathryn and why she had been away for an entire week, Clint thought. He frowned. "I still don't understand why you left Kathryn here. Don't you have family? A regular baby-sitter?'' He eyed her sternly. ''You took one hell of a chance, putting her on the porch and just walking away.''

''No family, and I didn't know what else to do,'' she exclaimed. ''As I was leaving the courtroom to go home to pack and make sure Kathryn's regular baby-sitter could watch her, a man sidled up next to me and threatened me—threatened Kathryn.'' Her blue eyes darkened as she remembered her fear.

Kathryn stirred against her, as if picking up the negative vibes her mother radiated. ''Shh,'' she soothed her daughter, and rubbed a fingertip across Kathryn's wrinkled brow. The baby instantly settled back into her peaceful slumber.

Mandy once again looked at Clint. ''He whispered in my ear, told me I had a beautiful baby, but if I didn't vote to acquit Maxwell Boothe, she wouldn't be beautiful for long.'' She looked down at the baby in her arms, and when she gazed at Clint, tears once again shimmered in her eyes.

''I didn't know what to do…where to turn. I wasn't willing to put Kathryn at risk, but I also wasn't willing to be blackmailed into anything.''

''And so you thought of Dave,'' Clint said.

She nodded. ''I went home and packed, then got up in the middle of the night and drove for hours, making certain I wasn't being followed. Then, just after dawn, I came here and left Kathryn.''

She looked at them both, pleading for them to

understand. "It was the only thing I could think of to remove her from harm so I could do what I had to do." She rubbed her forehead in a gesture of weariness. "Dave is rather immature and not ready for commitment or a family, but I knew he'd take good care of her. He's a good man at heart."

"The moment you were threatened you should have gone immediately to the judge or the prosecuting attorney," Clint said.

She eyed him cynically. "I was afraid to. I know that in the past, material witnesses against this man have disappeared, that even in one instance a witness under protection, hidden in a safe house, was killed. I didn't know who could really be trusted, so I decided to trust only myself."

"I would have done the same thing," Sherry replied, then looked at Clint defiantly. "Well, I would have, especially if it meant the safety of my child."

Clint wanted to protest, to tell them both that going to the authorities was the proper thing to do...the safe thing to do, but he was savvy enough to recognize that cops could be bought, as well as judges and attorneys.

"As soon as we returned the verdict, I told both the judge and the prosecuting attorney about the threat. I also gave them a physical description of the man and they immediately issued a warrant for his arrest," Mandy said.

"It was probably the same man who tried to

break in here and get to Kathryn,'' Clint said, thinking aloud.

Mandy gasped in horror. ''Somebody tried to break in, and you think they were after my daughter?''

''Yeah, but hopefully it's the man who threatened you, and before long the authorities will have him in custody,'' Clint tried to assure her.

Mandy nodded, although her grasp had once again tightened around her daughter. ''I'm taking Kathryn and going on a little vacation until all this has quieted down.''

''That's probably a good idea,'' Clint agreed.

''Does that mean you understand why I left her? That I'm free to take her and go?''

Clint looked at the sleeping little girl and studiously kept his gaze away from Sherry. He knew her heart was breaking, and he couldn't bear to see it happen right before his eyes. He nodded to Mandy. ''You're free to go.''

She stood, grateful tears spilling onto her cheeks. ''Can I pay you...for taking care of her?''

''No,'' Sherry said sharply and stood as well. ''There's no price that can be placed on our love. She has some things here. Just let me go get them.'' She turned on her heels and disappeared from the living room.

''I don't know how to thank you,'' Mandy said to Clint. ''I'll never be able to repay you for your kindness in keeping her here, taking care of her.''

"Keep her safe and love her, that's all we ask of you," Clint said, surprised to find a lump in his throat that made speech difficult.

Mandy nodded, her face reflecting the kind of steely strength and protective love that only a mother could possess.

Sherry came back into the room, clutching not only the diaper bag but a large shopping bag, as well. "These are the things you left with her," she said as she handed Mandy the diaper bag.

"And these are things Clint and I picked up for her. She loves to chew on the rattle that looks like a dancing bear, and the pink blanket is her favorite...." Sherry dropped the bag at Mandy's feet and turned away. "Please...excuse me. I'm sorry," she said, her voice trembling with tears. She turned and ran from the living room.

Clint helped Mandy carry everything to her car. He buckled Kathryn's seat into the back of her car, then gently placed the baby girl into the seat and buckled her in. He placed his lips against her sweet little cheek in a lingering final kiss.

A hollow ache resonated inside him as he watched the car pull away from the curb and disappear into the purple shadows of deep twilight. Finally the mystery of Kathryn had been solved, and she was now gone from their lives.

He turned and went back into the house, knowing somehow he had to help Sherry pick up the pieces of her heart. He walked through the living room, down the hallway and stopped outside her closed bedroom door.

He thought about knocking, but knew she'd turn him away. He knew instinctively that her grief was deep, almost as deep as the anguish she'd suffered when the doctor had told her she would have no children of her own.

She'd been reluctant to share her grief then, too. It had taken her three days before she'd allow him to hold her, allow his shoulder to absorb her tears, his heart to help carry the burden of her pain.

He opened the door to find her lying on the bed in the near-dark room. "Sherry," he called her name softly.

"Go away, Clint. I'll be out in a little while." Her voice was muffled by the pillow she clutched against her.

"No, darlin', I'm not going to go away." He sat on the edge of the bed. "I'm the one who's partially responsible for your hurting. I think the least I can do is help make the pain go away."

She started to protest, but he didn't give her a chance. He stretched out beside her and took her in his arms. She held herself stiff and unyielding for a moment, then relaxed against him as he stroked her back.

She was silent, but her body shook with sobs so deep they made no sound. He held her close, hoping to absorb some of her pain, hoping to transfer some measure of comfort.

Endless moments passed; the room was silent except for her occasional gasps for breath. He rubbed his hands up and down her back, letting her spill her grief against his chest.

"I'm sorry, Sherry," he said softly. "I should have never gotten you involved in all this."

"No...don't say that. I'll be all right with time." She drew a deep breath. "I loved her, Clint. I loved her with all my heart." Her features crumbled and this time when she cried, the sound of her weeping threatened to rip him apart.

When she finally pulled herself together, she pushed against his chest, distancing herself enough from him that she could look into his face. "I'm glad you got me involved. I wouldn't take back one minute of her smiles, her laughter, her funny little faces."

The light from a nearby streetlamp shone through the window, and in the pale illumination he saw her lips curve into a soft smile that stirred emotions deep inside him.

"It hurts, losing her," she said softly. "I knew all along it was inevitable, but Kathryn left me a tremendous gift."

"A gift?" Clint looked at her curiously, wondering if she had any idea how beautiful she looked in spite of her tear-stained features.

"She gave me back my gift of love. I thought I'd lost it. I've consciously avoided it, but Kathryn showed me that I can love a child who isn't mine."

Her face shone with the beauty of her discovery, and without a conscious decision being made, without any forethought involved, Clint covered her lips with his.

Sherry had no defenses against the warmth of his lips, the overwhelming desire to remain forever in his embrace. Sensations swept through her—desire, need, love.

She knew she should stop the kiss, pull away before those sensations carried her to a place where she could no longer halt the heat that had already begun to build between them.

Why halt anything? a little voice said in the back of her brain. Why not just this one night indulge all the love, all the desire you have inside you for Clint? For five long years you've wanted him. Why not indulge that want?

If she couldn't have a lifetime with him, at least she'd have the memory of one night of lovemaking with him. A memory to cherish, to hold close to her heart, a memory of love that would warm her through the years to come.

He moaned softly as her tongue danced with his, her hands rubbing up beneath his T-shirt to caress the hot skin beneath.

She pressed her body against the length of his and felt his desire for her in the taut, hard lines of his body. Heaven help her, but she wanted him.

His scent surrounded her, the spice of his cologne

mingling with the natural musk of his body and the faint lingering scent of minty soap. The combined fragrances caused a dizzy intoxication in her head, sending her desire to dazzling new heights.

"Sherry...my sweet Sherry," he murmured when his lips left hers and blazed a trail across her cheek and down the side of her neck.

His hands moved from her back to her sides, then continued upward until his palms cupped her breasts and his thumbs teased the hardened tips. Despite the material of her blouse and her bra, she could feel the heat that radiated from his touch, a provocative fire that threatened to consume her.

And she wanted to be consumed. She wanted to lose herself in his scent, lose herself to the touch and taste of him.

Moving her hips against his, she felt the way their bodies were intended to connect. Just this once, she told herself. Just give me this one time with Clint, let him be my first experience in love-making.

She pushed his shirt up, letting him know without words that she wanted him to take it off. With one graceful movement he pulled the shirt over his head and tossed it off the side of the bed.

Instantly Sherry explored his bare skin, reveling in the feel of his taut stomach, caressing upward to discover his bigger, harder chest muscles, then tangling her fingers in his wiry chest hair.

The room was no longer silent, but filled with

the sound of their breathing, their soft moans of pleasure as they kissed once again.

Sherry clung to him, wanting him to take her, possess her completely. She loved him so much it hurt inside, a hurt she knew she'd carry for the rest of her life.

"Sherry," he said softly as their lips finally parted. He framed her face with his hands, his eyes glowing in the semidarkness of the room. "We have to stop."

"No…no we don't," she protested. "I want you to make love to me. Please, Clint. Please make love to me."

He closed his eyes and remained unmoving. When he opened his eyes to look at her again, the flames of desire that had filled them before were gone. "No, Sherry. Not like this. This wasn't the way you wanted it."

She remembered all those nights so long ago. Always. Always it had been him who had possessed the strength to stop them before they actually made love.

His desire for her had apparently never been as intense as hers for him. And it seemed that hadn't changed.

Overwhelming anguish swept through her. Now she wouldn't even have the memory of one night with him to sustain her through the coming years. She couldn't even have that.

She remained unmoving on the bed as he rolled

away from her and reached out to turn on the small lamp next to the bed. The lamp created a small pool of intimate golden light.

His hair was tousled and his cheeks slightly flushed. The soft lighting emphasized his bare, tanned chest, and Sherry had never seen him look so achingly handsome.

She closed her eyes, not wanting to look at him, embarrassed by the fact she'd pled with him to take her, to make love to her, and he'd denied her.

"Sherry, marry me."

Her eyes jerked open at his words. She stared at him in disbelief, her heart leaping with both joy and despair. "What did you say?" she asked breathlessly.

"Marry me, Sherry. Spend your life with me." His eyes blazed with emotion. "I love you. I want to be your first lover...and your last."

Tears sprang to her eyes as her love for him filled her up. She wanted to say yes. She wanted to spend the rest of her life with him, make love to him each and every night of her existence. But she knew it would never work.

She rolled off the bed and stood, seeking some modicum of strength inside herself, needing to summon the fortitude to walk away from him. "I think we've both gotten confused by spending this past week together, pretending to be a family of sorts. It's been a rather pleasant fantasy, but just a fantasy nevertheless."

Walking over to the closet, she studiously avoided looking at him, knowing that if she gazed at him her resolve might weaken. She reached inside the closet and grabbed her suitcase.

"What are you doing?"

"Packing to go home." She finally turned to look at him. "Clint, we both knew I was just here for Kathryn. Now she's gone and it's time for me to go. I need to get back to my life."

"Sherry." He got off the bed and came to stand before her. "I'm not confused. I'm not delusional. I'm not lingering in any fantasy that might have taken place this past week. I love you. I want to marry you. I want you to be my wife. I want your life to be with me." His eyes searched her face.

She pushed past him and opened her suitcase on the bed. "Dammit, Sherry, listen to me," he exclaimed. He took her by the shoulders and whirled her around to face him. "Don't you hear what I'm telling you?"

"I hear you, Clint." She swallowed hard against the tears that threatened. She wouldn't cry. Not now. Not in front of him. Later she would cry all the tears of heartache she was holding back. "But it's foolish for us to even consider marrying. We want different things. We need different things."

She reached up and touched his cheek with trembling fingers. His eyes, those beautiful silvery-blue eyes were filled with a combination of emotions—love, anger, hurt…they were all there for her to see.

"Clint, you deserve a woman who can give you children of your own. I can't do that, but I won't live a life without children."

She dropped her hand from him. "From the time I was small all I dreamed about was having a child to nurture and raise. I declined dates and chose baby-sitting on Saturday nights. I went into the teaching profession because I love children. I meant it when I told you I intend to adopt, and we both know how you feel about that."

She stepped away from him and reached into the closet for a handful of hanging clothes and an additional dose of inner strength. "Eventually we'd grow to resent each other."

Efficiently she snagged the clothes off the hangers, folded them and placed them in the suitcase. "This past week was a nice fantasy, Clint."

"Stop saying that," he said, his voice husky and deep. "It wasn't just a nice fantasy. It was what I want the rest of my life to be like—us together, sharing the days, sharing the nights."

Sherry's heart cried out at the unfairness of it all. Why did they have to love each other, yet be so wrong for each other. "Please...don't make this difficult. Just let me go."

For a long moment they gazed at each other, then with a curt nod he turned and left the room, closing the door behind him.

With a strangled sob Sherry sat on the edge of the bed. She leaned down and picked up Clint's

T-shirt from the floor. She put it to her face and breathed deeply, anguish pressing heavily on her chest.

He loved her. She'd seen it in his eyes, felt it in his embrace, tasted it in each and every kiss they had shared. He loved her...and she had to walk away from that love.

She threw the shirt back on the floor and returned to her packing. How long would it hurt? How long would her love for Clint burn in her heart? How long before the pain finally faded, became more manageable?

Somehow, some way, fate had crossed their stars, letting them love each other, but not giving them the ingredients for happiness forever.

It wasn't fair. But Sherry had learned a long time ago that life wasn't fair.

It didn't take her long to finish packing her things. When she'd finished, she picked up her purse and her suitcase and left the bedroom.

Clint sat on the sofa, shoulders sagging in defeat. He looked up when she came into the room. "So, you're going," he stated flatly.

"It's time to go—time for both of us to move on with our lives." Her words sounded pretentious, yet created a hollow ache deep within her. "I'll call you," she said, recognizing it was a lie.

"Yeah, I'll see you around." He didn't move from his position.

Sherry hesitated a moment, wanting to say something, do something to make things better, but she knew there was nothing she could say, nothing she could do.

"Goodbye, Clint," she said softly, then stepped out the front door and into the darkness of the night.

She placed her suitcase in the back seat of the car, then slid behind the steering wheel. She put the key in the ignition, but didn't turn over the engine.

Instead she sat and stared at the house where for the past week she'd known happiness. It was a house just the right size for a family. And someday Clint would fill it with a wife and a baby or two.

She started her car and pulled away from the curb. When she looked in her rearview mirror, the house had disappeared, impossible to see amid the wash of her tears.

Chapter Nine

The next ten days were a curious blend of tremendous joy and devastating despair for Sherry. She tried to keep herself busy, her mind occupied. She tried to ignore how empty her apartment felt, how utterly alone she felt. Silence had become her enemy, allowing in too many painful thoughts of Clint.

For the first couple of days, she spent her time working on résumés to send out. She hoped to get back on as a teacher in the Armordale Elementary School but decided to hedge her bets and apply to some of the surrounding school districts as well.

With her résumés complete and in the mail, she then unpacked all the boxes that held her books and teaching supplies. As she unpacked the items that symbolized her brief life as a teacher, she was reminded of how much she'd loved that work.

She unpacked notes and little gifts from students, mourning the loss of the past five years. She'd loved working with children, loved seeing their eyes light with understanding when she taught them a new concept. She'd loved sharing their lives and being their helpmate. Thankfully it wasn't too late for her to go back to doing what she so loved.

With her positive new approach to work came no relief from the heartache of loving Clint. He was a song in her heart that would forever remain unsung, a lyrical poem that would never be written, and not a day went by that he wasn't an ache deep inside her.

She hadn't seen him for the past ten days, hadn't spoken to him at all. She picked up the phone a dozen times a day, just wanting to hear his voice, just needing to say hello. But she never completed any of the calls.

She mourned not only the fact that he wouldn't be her lover, would never be her husband, but also the fact that their friendship also had to be sacrificed for her own survival.

But today wasn't the day to dwell on heartache. Today was a joyous occasion. Today she was going to become the godmother to Kathryn Elaine Jenkins.

She stared at her reflection in her dresser mirror, still unable to believe that fate had allowed her to remain an integral part in the life of the child she had grown to love.

Mandy Jenkins had returned to Armordale two days after the night she'd left. She'd come to tell Sherry that the man who had threatened her had been arrested and had confessed that he'd attempted to break into Clint's house. With him safely behind bars, Mandy had decided to begin a new life in Armordale.

With no family, no real friends, she'd asked Sherry to be godmother, telling Sherry that she'd felt the love Sherry had for her daughter.

Sherry smiled, deciding that her peach-colored suit was a perfect choice for the day. Smart and chic, yet soft and sensual, the silky fabric clung to her curves without being tacky.

She turned away from the mirror and looked at her watch. She had a feeling more than half the town would be at church that morning to see little Kathryn baptized. In the week that Mandy and her daughter had claimed Armordale as home, the town had embraced the young mother and her smiling child.

Yes, it was a joyous day, with only one gray cloud on the horizon. Mandy had asked Clint to be Kathryn's godfather.

Today, during the church service, Clint and Sherry would sit side by side, then during Kathryn's baptism they would stand together and pledge their love and support for the little girl.

Somehow Sherry would have to survive being close to him, looking at him and smelling his familiar scent, and somehow she would hang on to her control.

She looked at her watch once again and realized it was time to go. She was both anticipating and dreading the day to come.

The church parking lot was already filling. Sherry found an empty space and parked her car. As she walked toward the church she nodded and waved to friends and neighbors.

Going to church was something else Sherry had allowed to fall out of her life. She'd been angry for so long—angry at fate and angry at God for her barrenness.

As she slid into the pew at the front, where Mandy had instructed her to sit, she embraced the familiar sights and smells.

Candles burned on the altar, and the floral arrangement sent its sweet fragrance into the air. Whispered murmurs of people greeting each other mingled with the soft organ music playing a familiar hymn.

Peace flooded through her, and she felt strong enough to handle anything…even Clint's presence.

She smiled with delight as Mandy, holding a white-gowned Kathryn, sat down next to her. Kathryn grinned and held out chubby arms to Sherry. Sherry laughed and took the smiling little girl onto her lap.

"I can't thank you enough for agreeing to this," Mandy said. "I'll rest easier each night knowing that if anything ever happens to me, Kathryn will have godparents who love her and will care for her."

Sherry grabbed Mandy's hand and squeezed. "Nothing is going to happen to you for many, many years to come. And thank you for sharing your daughter's life, your daughter's love with me." Sherry smiled at the young woman, who over the past week had become a friend.

"You doing okay?" Mandy asked with a note of concern. In a brief, weak moment Sherry had confessed to the young woman her heartache over Clint. "I hope this won't be, you know, too uncomfortable for you."

Sherry smiled reassuringly. "Don't worry. I'm fine, and nothing is going to spoil this day. Right sweet baby?" She kissed Kathryn on her chubby cheek, then laughed as the little girl clapped her hands together.

Both Sherry and Mandy looked up as Clint appeared before them. The strength Sherry was so certain would hold her in good stead, seeped out of her on a sigh.

He looked so tall, so handsome. He was clad in a navy suit with a crisp white shirt and his hair was neatly styled.

"Sherry...Mandy." He greeted the two women

with a nod, then squatted down in front of Kathryn. "And hello to you, little miss sunshine."

Kathryn reached out to him and with a nod of assent from Sherry, he took the little girl from her arms. As he whispered in Kathryn's ear, making her laugh, Sherry drank him in, gazing at each and every feature.

Although handsome as sin, he looked tired. Strain deepened the lines around his eyes and along the sides of his mouth.

As the organ music swelled, signaling the beginning of the service, Clint handed Kathryn back to her mother, then sat down next to Sherry.

Sherry tried to keep her thoughts focused on the sermon, but it was virtually impossible with Clint sitting so close to her she could feel the heat from his body. His scent surrounded her, making her heart ache with a renewed vengeance.

After the service she stood next to him and together they were recognized as the godparents to Kathryn Elaine Jenkins. The members of the congregation cheered, and then everyone began to spill out of the church and into the beautiful spring air.

As was customary, nobody hurried off, but rather the crowd lingered, greeting old friends, exchanging bits of gossip and enjoying the community spirit that prevailed all around.

Sherry stood with Clint, Mandy and Kathryn, accepting the well wishes of friends and neighbors. She and Clint exchanged looks of surprise as Walt

Clary shuffled over to say hello, Betty Wade on his arm.

Clint nodded in greeting. "Betty...Walt...nice of the two of you to put your homicidal tendencies toward each other on hold long enough to attend church together."

Walt snorted. "We made a truce. She's going to try to train Rover." He leaned closer to Clint and winked conspiratorially. "Although I got a feeling she's trying to do a little training on me, too."

"Don't worry, Walt," Clint said as he slapped the old man on the back. "I've heard tell that you can't teach an old dog new tricks."

"That's what you think," Betty said with a wink of her own. She grabbed Walt's arm. "Come on, Walt. You're taking me out to lunch at the café."

Sherry watched in amazement as the two walked away arm in arm. "I swear, I think I actually saw Walt smile," she said.

Without warning, Clint took her by the arm and pulled her aside from everyone else. "Sherry...we need to talk. It's important."

She pulled her arm from his grasp, the simplest touch from him sheer torture. "We have nothing to talk about," she objected.

"Please, take a drive with me. Just give me a few minutes of your time." His eyes bored into hers, compelling, demanding and oddly vulnerable all at the same time. "Sherry, please...there are some things I need to tell you, some things I need to explain.''

She knew she should say no, that to go anywhere with him, to have any conversation with him was nothing short of madness. But he'd managed to intrigue her. Before she knew what she was doing, she nodded her assent.

Within minutes they were in his car, driving to the outskirts of town. "Where are we going?" she asked.

"To the lake," he said.

A ringing note of dread resounded in Sherry's stomach. The lake—the place where they had spent so many happy hours, the place where he had proposed to her so long ago.

She closed her eyes, wishing she were anywhere but here, knowing that nothing was ahead of her but more pain.

Clint drove slowly, trying to gather his thoughts before they got to the lake. In just a few minutes he intended to have the most painful discussion he'd ever had with anyone in his life.

He was going to explore pain he'd shoved in the deepest recesses of his mind, delve into a past that held incredible anguish.

But he hoped it would all be worth it. He would pay with his pain if it meant he and Sherry might somehow find a future together.

"Clint...I don't think this is such a good idea,"

she said, breaking into his reverie. "Why do we have to go to the lake? We could have talked at the church."

"No, it has to be at the lake. That's where it all began." He cast her a quick glance. "That's where I first told you I love you. It seems fitting that the lake is where we'll finish it all."

She sighed heavily. "Clint, we finished it the night I left your house."

"No, we didn't. Just trust me, I have some things to say that are important...things you have a right to know."

They fell silent, and Clint could feel her tension filling the interior of the car. He cast her a surreptitious glance, and his heart expanded with his love for her.

She looked so beautiful. The peach-colored suit pulled matching color into her cheeks and deepened the green of her eyes. Her short hair was a curly cap of shiny strands, slightly tossed by the wind to give her a sexy, just-out-of-bed kind of look.

He tightened his grip on the steering wheel. He had no idea how she would react when he told her what he needed to say. Sherry had never liked people who lied, and for over the past five years Clint had lived a lie of sorts.

It was possible she would hear what he had to say and turn away, forever shutting him out of her life. Or it was possible with the secret out they might be able to build a life together after all. God, he hoped it was the latter. He didn't want to live another day without her in his life.

He parked the car on the south side of the lake, in the exact same spot where they had always parked for an hour or two of quiet talk and necking.

When he shut off the engine, he rolled down his window and Sherry did the same, allowing a cross breeze of fresh, clean air to drift through the car.

With all his previous pondering, he still didn't know exactly where to begin. He slid his seat back, released his seat belt, then turned to look at her, loving her with his eyes, hoping, praying she might love him back.

"These last ten days have been horrible for me," he began. "I never knew my house could be so quiet—suffocatingly quiet."

She nodded. "I know what you mean. My apartment feels the same way." She folded her hands in her lap and stared straight ahead out the car window. "But that's just because we got used to being together, and having Kathryn fill us up with laughter."

Clint shook his head. "I'll agree that Kathryn's absence made a difference, but, Sherry, it was you I missed. I missed waking up each morning and knowing you were the first adult I was going to see. I missed sharing my first cup of coffee of the day with you sitting across from me at the table."

He reached out and took her hand in his, forcing her to look at him. "In the past ten days I've missed you being the last person I see, the last person I talk to before I go to sleep."

"Is this what was so important that you tell me?" She withdrew her hand from his.

"No, it's not." He drew a deep breath and raked a hand through his hair. For a long moment he stared out the window at the placid surface of the lake, once again seeking the right words to speak. "Sherry, my parents aren't dead."

She gasped and he turned to look at her once again. "What are you talking about? Of course your parents are dead. You told me they died in a car accident before you moved to Armordale."

"My real parents died in a car accident when I was two. The people who actually raised me are alive and well and living in Kansas City."

He watched the play of emotions on her face as she slowly digested his words. "You were adopted?" she finally asked.

He nodded. "I was three when Robert and Mary Graham adopted me. I was lucky, that's what everyone told me, to be adopted by such a fine couple." He tried to keep the bitterness out of his voice, but couldn't. "Robert owns a couple of banks, and Mary is devoted to her charity work. Oh yes, I was damned lucky to be adopted by such a prominent couple."

The memories of his childhood rose up inside him, memories he'd spent his adult life trying to forget. He opened his car door, needing more fresh air than the windows could provide. "Let's take a walk." He got out of the car and waited for her to join him.

They began to walk around the edge of the lake where a graveled path had been provided by the city. "Clint...I don't understand. Why did you lie about this? Why didn't you just tell me you were adopted?"

The sun on his shoulders was warm, but the icy wind of unwanted memories ripped through him. "Because when I left Kansas City, I wanted to forget everything about those people and my childhood."

"Was it that bad?" she whispered, her heart full of pain on his behalf.

He nodded curtly. "Not a day went by that they didn't make me feel inadequate, that they didn't remind me that they didn't have to love me because I wasn't their natural-born son. When I was bad, it was because I wasn't really theirs. When I was good, it was due to their influence raising me above my innate badness."

"Oh, Clint," she replied softly, and reached for his hand.

He closed his eyes for a moment and allowed the warmth of her hand to assuage the pain of the child he had been. He opened his eyes to gaze at her, knowing his pain shone from his eyes. "Every day of my life I hated being adopted, hated how they made me feel I'd never be good enough. I grew up knowing that nothing I could do, nothing I could say would ever really make them love me because I hadn't been born to them.''

"And that's why you never wanted to adopt any children," she said, understanding lighting her eyes. "You were afraid you'd do to an adopted child what was done to you."

He offered her a bitter smile. "I learned my parenting skills from Mr. and Mrs. Dysfunctional. I not only didn't want to adopt, I also never considered having children of my own." He smoothed a hand through his hair. "They're such fragile creatures and so easily wounded."

They stopped walking and he stood before her, needing to ask her something that had gnawed at his heart for the past five years. "Sherry, now I need to understand something from you."

"What?" She looked at him curiously.

"When you found out you couldn't have children, why did you break off our engagement?" His throat closed with emotion. "Why wasn't I enough for you?"

She stared at him, her eyes widened. She shook her head slowly side to side, her gaze not leaving his. "Oh, Clint, it was never about you not being enough. It was about me not being enough."

This time it was Sherry who once again began to walk, as if she was now dealing with her own inner pain and needed the activity of pacing.

"When I discovered I couldn't have children,

something inside of me died." She drew a deep breath, then continued, "I somehow lost the ability to love at all. You deserved more than what I could give you, and I thought the kindest thing I could do was let you go."

He stopped her by stepping in front of her. "It wasn't a kind thing. You broke my heart, stole my dream of living with you, loving you for the rest of my life."

She smiled, a sad expression that did nothing to light up her features. "And now we're back at the same place, with the same obstacles standing between us."

She reached up and touched his cheek, the simple touch transmitting her heart to him. "Only now I understand why you never wanted to consider adoption." She dropped her hand and shrugged. "Stalemate."

"No, not stalemate." He took her by the shoulders. "Sherry, today while I stood beside you and pledged my love for Kathryn, something amazing happened. I loved her when I thought she was mine, and I believed my love for her had changed when I realized she wasn't mine. But as I looked at her sweet little face, remembered all the moments we shared in the week we had her, I realized I still loved her with all my heart and it didn't matter that she hadn't come from me."

Sherry's lovely eyes locked with his, and she

stepped away from him. Her body seemed to vibrate with intensity. "Wh-what are you saying?"

"I'm saying that I love you, and if you want to adopt a child, then I want to be its father.... I want to be the kind of father I never had." He laughed. "Hell, I know all the ways not to be a father."

"But I watched you with Kathryn," she reminded him. "And I know you also know all the ways to be a wonderful father."

Once again he took her by the shoulders and drew her closer to him. "Marry me, Sherry. Marry me and live your life with me. We'll build a family together and make our dreams come true."

Her eyes filled with tears, but he could tell by the light shining in their green depths that they were tears of happiness. "You mean it?"

He laughed and drew her into an embrace. "I've never meant anything more. Now, are you going to marry me and put us both out of our misery?"

"Yes, oh, yes," she said, and she raised up on tiptoe as their mouths met in a kiss that spoke of the promise of dreams fulfilled, the heat of passion unleashed and the wonder of love forevermore.

Chapter Ten

"**D**arling, you look beautiful." Sherry's mother, Nadine, clapped her hands together in delight as Sherry stood before her in her wedding gown.

She kissed Sherry's cheek, then grasped her hands. "I can't tell you how happy I am for you, that finally you've found happiness with a man you love. I hope today is the first day of a wonderful new life for you."

Sherry squeezed her mother's hands. "And I can't thank you enough for working so hard to pull this wedding together so quickly."

It had been only three weeks since Sherry and Clint had stood by the edge of the lake and Sherry had told Clint she would marry him.

Nadine laughed. "That man of yours is an impatient one. If he'd had his way, this wedding would have taken place two weeks ago." She released Sherry's hands and instead busied herself arranging the fine netting of Sherry's veil over Sherry's face.

Sherry stood patiently, although her heart pounded with anticipation. In just a few minutes she would become Clint's wife. Her pulse raced, and every nerve in her body felt electrified.

She felt as if she'd fallen into the most wonderful dream she'd ever experienced and she never, ever wanted to awaken.

The first day of a wonderful new life—a life to be spent loving Clint. The loneliness, the unhappiness of five years had melted away with the kiss she and Clint had shared on the day she'd agreed to marry him.

The past three weeks had been busy as the couple had prepared for the wedding and made decisions about Sherry's apartment furnishings. They'd moved the things she wanted to keep into Clint's house, creating a household of furniture and kitchen items that blended their two lives. Sherry had moved out of her apartment and in with her mother for the past several days.

And tonight—she shivered as she thought about the night to come. Her wedding night. The night she would share her first experience of making love with the man she loved.

A knock sounded on the door, and Sherry's sister stepped inside. "Oh, Sis, you look positively stunning," she exclaimed. "They sent me to tell you that it's time."

As Sherry, her sister and her mother left the church nursery, which had served as their dressing room, Sherry's stomach fluttered nervously.

Within hours she would be alone with Clint. What if she wasn't good at making love? Maybe they would have been smart to have made love before the wedding, to be certain they were a good fit in that respect. She was completely inexperienced. What if Clint was disappointed in her? She clutched her bouquet of baby's breath and yellow roses, hoping she didn't throw up before she ever managed to say, "I do."

She took her place at the back of the church, vaguely aware that it was a full house. It appeared that all of Armordale had turned out to see their sheriff married.

What if she was frigid? The terrible thought intruded into her mind. What if she really was no good at making love and Clint decided he'd made a horrible mistake? She would die. She would absolutely, positively curl up and die of heartache.

The church organ swelled with the familiar notes to the "Wedding March" and tears of fear burned behind her eyes. As she started her walk up the aisle, her gaze sought Clint.

He stood at the other end of the aisle, tall and handsome in a black tuxedo. As she drew closer, she saw his eyes, and they were filled with love.

All the fear that had momentarily claimed her fled, unable to sustain itself beneath the utter glory in his eyes.

When she reached him, he took her hand in his. She knew hers was icy cold, but it warmed beneath the heat of his. He smiled, and she knew at that very moment that everything was going to be just fine.

The ceremony flew by in a haze. Vows were spoken, rings were exchanged and a kiss sealed the future. The crowd left the church and went to the community center for the reception.

The interior of the community center had been decorated with crepe paper, and a long table held punch and a three-tier wedding cake. A band was tuning up on the small stage, and additional food was laid out on another large table.

For the next thirty minutes Clint and Sherry stood side by side by the front door, accepting the best wishes and sly winks of friends and neighbors.

"Have I told you lately that I love you?" Clint asked when they finally found themselves alone for a moment.

She smiled up at him. "Probably, but tell me again. You know how I love to hear it."

He pulled her against him. "I love you," he said, and pressed his lips to hers in a kiss that contained fiery passion and a hunger for the night to come.

"Hey, now," Andy said, interrupting the moment. "Let's not be starting the honeymoon too soon. Come on, everybody is waiting for you two to have the first dance.''

Clint smiled at Sherry. ''Mrs. Graham, may I have this dance?''

She thrilled at the sound of her new name. ''Why certainly, Mr. Graham,'' she replied.

And then she was in his arms, moving to the strains of a soft, romantic song as the crowd cheered. Within minutes other couples twirled onto the floor, and Sherry and Clint were no longer the center of attention.

''You look so beautiful, you take my breath away,'' he said, and his words combined with the flames in his eyes and stole her breath away.

For the next hour or so they danced, they fed each other cake and did all the traditional things that were done at wedding receptions.

Sherry was visiting with Mandy and Kathryn when Clint came up behind her. ''Let's blow this party,'' he whispered in her ear. Sherry felt the heat of a blush warm her cheeks as Mandy laughed.

''Go. The bride and groom never stay too long at their reception,'' she agreed, earning herself a grateful smile from Clint.

Clint took Sherry by the hand and led her toward the door. ''Shouldn't we tell somebody goodbye? Tell everyone thank you?'' she asked.

''No, we should sneak out quietly and let them all party without us.'' He pulled her out the door and toward his car. They both stopped short and laughed as they saw the tin cans tied to the bumper, Just Married written in white across the sides and back window.

Andy was in the process of tying a big white bow on the antenna. He grinned at them as they approached. "You two lovebirds sneaking out of here?"

"You about done messing up my car?" Clint grinned at his deputy.

Andy gave the bow a final pat and nodded. "Yeah, I reckon I'm done. Now I don't want you worrying about anything while you're honeymooning." He drew a breath, expanding his chest broadly. "I can take care of the needs of this town for the next three days with no problem at all."

Clint slapped Andy on the back. "I wouldn't be taking three days off if I didn't have total confidence in you." A smile lit Andy's features at his boss's words.

Clint helped Sherry into the passenger side, then with a final goodbye to Andy, he slid behind the wheel. As he started the engine, all the nervous thoughts Sherry had entertained before suddenly reappeared.

"Where are we going?" she asked as he pulled away from the church. He'd told her he was taking her someplace special for their wedding night, but he hadn't said where. Each time she'd asked, his eyes had sparkled as he told her it was a secret.

He smiled, but did not reply. Instead he reached

over and took her hand in his. She looked at her hand, the fourth finger now adorned with a diamond wedding band. The diamonds sparkled and shone with each streetlight they passed.

"Happy?" he asked.

She nodded. "It all feels like a dream." She hesitated a moment, then asked, "Are you terribly disappointed?" She had insisted they invite his adoptive parents to the wedding, but they had not acknowledged the invitation and hadn't shown up at the ceremony.

"Disappointed? Oh, you mean about Robert and Mary? No, I'm not disappointed they didn't show and I'm not surprised." He squeezed her hand, then released it. "Maybe they were the best parents they knew how to be. I can finally forgive them, but that doesn't mean I want them in my life."

Sherry heard the peace in his voice, knew that in the past three weeks a healing had taken place inside Clint's heart where his past was concerned. She looked up in surprise as they pulled into his driveway.

He shut off the engine, released his seat belt and turned to her. "I hope you didn't have visions of some fancy hotel room for our wedding night." Once again he reached for her hand. "I wanted our first time to be here...in my bed, where I've dreamed of making love to you so many nights."

Tears momentarily blurred Sherry's vision as her love for this man welled up inside her, filling her with a completeness she'd never known. "I love you," she whispered.

His eyes flamed. "Let's go inside and let me show you just how much I love you."

Twenty minutes later Sherry stood in front of the bathroom mirror, staring at her reflection and fighting the fear that somehow Clint would find her an inadequate lover.

She wore a white silk gown that did little to cover her nakedness beneath. Her cheeks were flushed and her eyes appeared huge. It was time.

She drew a deep breath to try to still the nerves that shivered inside her, then opened the door and walked down the hallway toward Clint's bedroom.

He was there, already in bed—a bed covered with rose petals. A bottle of champagne chilled in an ice bucket next to two crystal glasses on the nightstand. The room smelled of the fragrant flowers and of Clint, a heady combination that threatened to buckle her knees.

"You look stunning," he said softly.

She didn't move from the doorway, hesitant as to what was expected of her. He patted the side of the bed next to him. "Come on, sweetheart. Let's drink a toast to our future."

She knew his gesture was intended to help her relax, and she smiled gratefully and moved to the side of the bed. As she slid beneath the covers, he poured them each a glass of the champagne.

"Champagne and rose petals...what more could a girl want?" she said, smiling nervously.

"Darlin', this is just the beginning," he replied and laughed as a blush stole across her features. He handed her a glass of the pink bubbly, then gently clinked his glass against hers. "To us. May we love each other and remain soul mates forever."

"Forever," she echoed softly. She took a sip of the fizzing drink, and he took a drink of his. Then, eyes gleaming, he took the glass from her and placed them both back on the nightstand.

Sherry's breath caught in her chest as he reached for her and pulled her into his arms. He was naked beneath the sheets, and she felt the warmth, the bold masculinity of him as she never had before.

Her heart, her body, her very soul melted as his lips claimed hers in a fiery kiss of hunger. The voracity of his kiss overwhelmed her. When he finally gave her a moment to breathe, tears shimmered in her eyes.

"Sherry, sweetheart...what's wrong?" he asked, his handsome features twisted into a frown of worry.

"I'm scared," she confessed, then emitted a nervous laugh. "What if I do something wrong? What if you don't like making love to me?"

"Darlin', that's not about to happen," he soothed, at the same time raining sweet butterfly kisses along her jawline. "We're going to make love beautifully, and there is no way I'm not going to love each and every moment of it."

He looked deep into her eyes. "Trust me, Sherry. I promise I won't hurt you, and I promise I won't ever stop loving you. Nothing you could ever do would make me stop loving you."

She saw the truth shining from his silvery-blue eyes, and the fear that had plagued her off and on for the past three weeks slid away.

Shyly she ran her hands across his broad, naked chest, then leaned forward and let her lips follow the trail her fingers blazed. She felt his swift intake of breath, and in the next instant desire exploded fully between them.

As his mouth sought hers again, he pushed the blankets off them and slowly slid her gown up her body. Slowly, sensually, he caressed each and every inch of skin he uncovered.

He seduced her...slowly, languidly, teaching her about her body while softly instructing her about his own. It was a give and take between them, a loving, learning process, as each memorized what the other liked, what caress caused sighs of pleasure, moans of delight.

When he finally entered her, she was eager and ready and there was no pain, only pleasure—a pleasure deeper, higher, sweeter than any she'd ever before experienced.

Afterward she lay in his arms, waiting for their

bodies to cool, waiting for their breathing to return to normal.

"I can't believe we waited five years to be together," she finally said.

He stroked a hand down her bare back, sending shivers up and down her spine. "I'm glad we waited," he replied.

She rose up and looked at him in surprise. "You are?"

He smiled. "I'm not glad we waited five long years, but I am glad we waited until our wedding night. I'm glad I got to be your first, and I'm determined to be your only, your last lover."

"I'm glad, too." She snuggled back against him, knowing she would never tire of being held in his arms, of being kissed by his lips. "Are we supposed to go to sleep now?"

"Only if you're tired," he replied. His hand slid up her side, resting teasingly just beneath her breast. "Are you tired?"

Her breath caught and she gasped as his hand no longer teased, but rather covered her breast warmly. "I'm not a bit tired," she said breathlessly.

"Good. After waiting five long years for you, I'm not near ready to bring this night to an end." He kissed her, and to her amazement, although she'd believed herself completely sated, she felt the stir of excitement once again.

"Hmm, remind me to buy Kathryn the best, biggest, most wonderful birthday present in the world," he murmured.

"Okay," she said. "Why would you think about that right now?"

He smiled at her and stroked a thumb down the curve of her jaw. "Because without the help of that precious little girl, two fools might have gone another five years before realizing they belonged together."

Epilogue

"Sherry?" Clint called as he walked through the front door of their home. He tossed the large greeting card he carried onto the coffee table.

"In the kitchen," she replied.

Clint walked into the kitchen to see his bride of one year leaning over to check something in the oven. He walked up behind her and wrapped his arms around her waist.

"Stop," she protested with a laugh, then whirled around to face him. He didn't release his hold on her. "You're home early," she observed.

"It's a special day," he answered. "I figure the sheriff is allowed to take off early on his one-year anniversary." He frowned as he saw the smothered steak baking in the oven. "I thought I was taking you out to dinner."

"I thought an intimate candlelight dinner for two would be nicer," she replied, her eyes sparkling with an inviting warm light.

"You vixen," he said with a laugh. "I know what you really have in mind...you intend to wine and dine me, then seduce me until I'm utterly senseless."

"Exactly," she agreed.

Clint sought her lips with his, amazed that after a full year of marriage, his desire, his love for her had only managed to increase. She returned his kiss with fervor, tangling her hands in his hair and pressing into him as if she couldn't get close enough.

Instantly Clint was aroused. He'd been delighted to discover that in making love to Sherry that first time, he'd apparently opened inside her a well of healthy, earthy, sweet passion. And it humbled him that her passion was provoked by him, intended only for him.

"Now, that's enough," she said breathlessly as the kiss ended. Her cheeks were flushed a pretty pink as she pushed him away and stepped away from his embrace. "Let me get the table set."

He took his seat and watched while she got out the good linen cloth and spread it over the oak table. As she got the good dishes out of the cabinet and began to place them, he smiled with the pleasure of a man who loved and was loved. "You don't have any students tonight, do you?"

She grinned at him. "Sure, I scheduled half a

dozen sessions so we couldn't spend our anniversary together.'' She laughed at his look of panic. ''Of course I don't have any students this evening.''

Sherry hadn't gotten a teaching job. There had been no openings available in any of the nearby districts. Instead she had begun an in-home tutoring service for children with learning disabilities and students who needed just a little extra help and encouragement.

Clint checked his watch, then got up and left the kitchen. He grabbed the large envelope he'd tossed on the coffee table and returned to the kitchen. ''Here, this is for you,'' he said as he held it out to Sherry.

Her eyes lit with pleasure. ''Oh, an anniversary card,'' she said. She opened the envelope and pulled out the flowery card. He watched her as she read it, saw the puzzled frown that momentarily crossed her forehead.

She looked back up at him. ''Honey, it's a beautiful sentiment, but did you realize it's a Mother's Day card, not an anniversary card?''

''Really?'' He feigned surprise as he took the card from her and pretended to scan the contents. ''Well, imagine that. I guess that just means that I need to make sure you're a mother today.'' He watched her, the utter stillness that overtook her, the tentative hope that lit her beautiful eyes.

He smiled and tossed the card aside so he could pull her into his arms. ''Nancy called today.''

"She has a baby for us?" Sherry's voice quivered with emotion.

Clint nodded and watched tears sparkle in her eyes. "A baby boy. We're supposed to meet her in her office in fifteen minutes."

"Fifteen minutes?" Sherry reeled out of his arms, her hands going to her hair, racing down the front of her. "But...but I can't go like this. I need to change clothes, put on some makeup." Despite her frantic words, she didn't move, and Clint laughed.

"Darlin', he's four weeks old. He won't care whether your hair is combed or you're wearing your Sunday finery." He took her hand in his. "Come on, let's go get our son."

Exactly fifteen minutes later they pulled up in front of the law office of Nancy Coltron. They had contacted Nancy soon after their wedding, explaining to the attractive, intelligent woman that they wanted to adopt.

Clint took Sherry's hand as they entered the office. Nancy sat in the waiting room, and Clint's heart plummeted as he saw no sign of a baby anywhere.

"Ah, two of my favorite people," Nancy said in greeting. "Please, sit down." She gestured them to the two chairs next to her.

"Has something happened? Is something wrong?" Clint asked. He felt the pressure of

Sherry's hand squeezing his. Please don't disappoint her, he prayed.

"Everything is wonderfully right," Nancy replied. "There are just a few things we need to discuss before I introduce you to your new son."

Clint and Sherry sat, but Clint didn't release her hand. He watched her face, felt her happiness and knew this was the most right thing they had ever done.

"I've never felt so good about an adoption before. This is pretty cut-and-dried. The parents are not confused young people, but rather a professional couple who don't want children. Little Scott was a mistake."

"Scott." Sherry breathed the name reverently. "Scott Graham." She looked at Clint, her eyes shining. "It has a wonderful ring to it, doesn't it?"

He nodded, completely filled with her happiness.

"The parents have already signed away their parental rights, so we can immediately petition the court and get the adoption process started." Nancy smiled at the two of them. "Congratulations. I truly believe the three of you belong together." She stood and smiled. "I'll be right back." She disappeared into her inner office and returned a moment later carrying a tiny bundle of blue.

Sherry and Clint met her halfway across the room and Clint watched as Sherry took the sleeping little boy from Nancy. "Oh, Clint. He's beautiful. Look how tiny he is.'' Sherry's voice quavered, and tears of joy trembled on her lashes.

Clint looked at the baby. Dark tufts of hair covered his head and long, dark lashes lay on chubby little cheeks. His little mouth pursed as if trying to blow a kiss, and emotion roared through Clint.

''Here, you hold him,'' Sherry said.

''No, I...'' Clint's protest fell away as she handed him the warm, tiny bundle. The baby squinted and opened one eye, then the other. For a moment he appeared to stare at Clint, as if contemplating whether or not Clint measured up.

The baby yawned widely, then closed his eyes once again, as if deciding Clint was fit for fatherhood. Love swelled inside Clint. It filled him up and brought tears to his eyes. Scott. His son.

''Here, I've got a present for you.'' Nancy pulled an infant car seat from her office. ''Now, go on, get out of here and take your son with you. I'll be in touch about the paperwork later.''

Clint handed Scott back to Sherry, his vision blurred with his tears of joy. He kissed his wife, then kissed his son's forehead. He picked up the car seat and held the door open for his wife and his son. Complete. They were a family now. ''Come on, let's go home,'' he said.

As they walked out to the car, Nancy called after them. ''Let me know when you're ready for Scott to have a sister or a brother.''

''It looks as if we're going to spend our anniversary shopping for baby things,'' Sherry said as they drove home.

''I can't think of anything I'd rather do,'' Clint replied, then grinned wickedly. ''Well, maybe I can think of one other thing I'd rather do.''

Sherry slapped him on the arm and laughed—a laugh that contained so much happiness, such complete joy, it warmed Clint's heart. Her laughter faded and she looked at him. ''Thank you, Clint. All my dreams are coming true, and it's all because of you.''

Clint smiled. ''And my dream came true the day you became my wife. Little Scott is just the icing on my cake.'' He pulled over to the side of the road and turned to her. ''But I want you to understand something,'' he said teasingly. ''Our second anniversary doesn't mean twins.''

She laughed and met him halfway for a kiss—a kiss that whispered of their love, their commitment and a future filled with joy.

* * * * *

Don't miss Carla Cassidy's
riveting romance, IN A HEARTBEAT,
on sale May 2000, only from
Silhouette Intimate Moments.

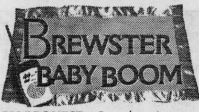

If you enjoyed what you just read,
then we've got an offer you can't resist!

Take 2 bestselling love stories FREE!
Plus get a FREE surprise gift!

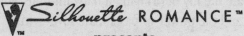

Soldiers of Fortune...prisoners of love.

Back by popular demand, international bestselling author **Diana Palmer**'s *daring and dynamic* Soldiers of Fortune *return!*

*Don't miss these unforgettable romantic classics in our wonderful 3-in-1 keepsake collection. Available in April 2000.**

And look for a **brand-new** *Soldiers of Fortune* tale in May. Silhouette Romance presents the next book in this riveting series:

MERCENARY'S WOMAN

(SR #1444)

She was in danger and he fought to protect her. But sweet-natured Sally Johnson dreamed of spending forever in Ebenezer Scott's powerful embrace. Would she walk down the aisle as this tender mercenary's bride?

Then in January 2001, look for THE WINTER SOLDIER in Silhouette Desire!

Available at your favorite retail outlet.
**Also available on audio from Brilliance.*

Silhouette®
Where love comes alive™

SILHOUETTE'S 20TH ANNIVERSARY CONTEST
OFFICIAL RULES
NO PURCHASE NECESSARY TO ENTER

1. To enter, follow directions published in the offer to which you are responding. Contest begins 1/1/00 and ends on 8/24/00 (the "Promotion Period"). Method of entry may vary. Mailed entries must be postmarked by 8/24/00, and received by 8/31/00.

2. During the Promotion Period, the Contest may be presented via the Internet. Entry via the Internet may be restricted to residents of certain geographic areas that are disclosed on the Web site. To enter via the Internet, if you are a resident of a geographic area in which Internet entry is permissible, follow the directions displayed on-line, including typing your essay of 100 words or fewer telling us "Where In The World Your Love Will Come Alive." On-line entries must be received by 11:59 p.m. Eastern Standard time on 8/24/00. Limit one e-mail entry per person, household and e-mail address per day, per presentation. If you are a resident of a geographic area in which entry via the Internet is permissible, you may, in lieu of submitting an entry on-line, enter by mail, by hand-printing your name, address, telephone number and contest number/name on an 8"x 11" plain piece of paper and telling us in 100 words or fewer "Where In The World Your Love Will Come Alive," and mailing via first-class mail to: Silhouette 20th Anniversary Contest, (in the U.S.) P.O. Box 9069, Buffalo, NY 14269-9069; (In Canada) P.O. Box 637, Fort Erie, Ontario, Canada L2A 5X3. Limit one 8"x 11" mailed entry per person, household and e-mail address per day. <u>On-line and/or 8"x 11" mailed entries received from persons residing in geographic areas in which Internet entry is not permissible will be disqualified.</u> No liability is assumed for lost, late, incomplete, inaccurate, nondelivered or misdirected mail, or misdirected e-mail, for technical, hardware or software failures of any kind, lost or unavailable network connection, or failed, incomplete, garbled or delayed computer transmission or any human error which may occur in the receipt or processing of the entries in the contest.

3. Essays will be judged by a panel of members of the Silhouette editorial and marketing staff based on the following criteria:

   Sincerity (believability, credibility)—50%
   Originality (freshness, creativity)—30%
   Aptness (appropriateness to contest ideas)—20%

   Purchase or acceptance of a product offer does not improve your chances of winning. In the event of a tie, duplicate prizes will be awarded.

4. All entries become the property of Harlequin Enterprises Ltd., and will not be returned. Winner will be determined no later than 10/31/00 and will be notified by mail. Grand Prize winner will be required to sign and return Affidavit of Eligibility within 15 days of receipt of notification. Noncompliance within the time period may result in disqualification and an alternative winner may be selected. All municipal, provincial, federal, state and local laws and regulations apply. Contest open only to residents of the U.S. and Canada who are 18 years of age or older, and is void wherever prohibited by law. Internet entry is restricted solely to residents of those geographical areas in which Internet entry is permissible. Employees of Torstar Corp., their affiliates, agents and members of their immediate families are not eligible. Taxes on the prizes are the sole responsibility of winners. Entry and acceptance of any prize offered constitutes permission to use winner's name, photograph or other likeness for the purposes of advertising, trade and promotion on behalf of Torstar Corp. without further compensation to the winner, unless prohibited by law. Torstar Corp and D.L. Blair, Inc., their parents, affiliates and subsidiaries, are not responsible for errors in printing or electronic presentation of contest or entries. In the event of printing or other errors which may result in unintended prize values or duplication of prizes, all affected contest materials or entries shall be null and void. If for any reason the Internet portion of the contest is not capable of running as planned, including infection by computer virus, bugs, tampering, unauthorized intervention, fraud, technical failures, or any other causes beyond the control of Torstar Corp. which corrupt or affect the administration, secrecy, fairness, integrity or proper conduct of the contest, Torstar Corp. reserves the right, at its sole discretion, to disqualify any individual who tampers with the entry process and to cancel, terminate, modify or suspend the contest or the Internet portion thereof. In the event of a dispute regarding an on-line entry, the entry will be deemed submitted by the authorized holder of the e-mail account submitted at the time of entry. Authorized account holder is defined as the natural person who is assigned to an e-mail address by an Internet access provider, on-line service provider or other organization that is responsible for arranging e-mail address for the domain associated with the submitted e-mail address.

5. Prizes: Grand Prize—a $10,000 vacation to anywhere in the world. Travelers (at least one must be 18 years of age or older) or parent or guardian if one traveler is a minor, must sign and return a Release of Liability prior to departure. Travel must be completed by December 31, 2001, and is subject to space and accommodations availability. Two hundred (200) Second Prizes—a two-book limited edition autographed collector set from one of the Silhouette Anniversary authors: Nora Roberts, Diana Palmer, Linda Howard or Annette Broadrick (value $10.00 each set). All prizes are valued in U.S. dollars.

6. For a list of winners (available after 10/31/00), send a self-addressed, stamped envelope to: Harlequin Silhouette 20th Anniversary Winners, P.O. Box 4200, Blair, NE 68009-4200.

Contest sponsored by Torstar Corp., P.O. Box 9042, Buffalo, NY 14269-9042.

PS20RULES

ENTER FOR A CHANCE TO WIN*

Silhouette's 20th Anniversary Contest

Tell Us Where in the World You Would Like *Your* Love To Come Alive... And We'll Send the Lucky Winner There!

Silhouette wants to take you wherever your happy ending can come true.

Here's how to enter: Tell us, in 100 words or less, where you want to go to make your love come alive!

In addition to the grand prize, there will be 200 runner-up prizes, collector's-edition book sets autographed by one of the Silhouette anniversary authors: **Nora Roberts, Diana Palmer, Linda Howard** or **Annette Broadrick**.

DON'T MISS YOUR CHANCE TO WIN! ENTER NOW! No Purchase Necessary

Silhouette®

Where love comes alive™

Name: _____

Address: _____

City: _____ State/Province: _____

Zip/Postal Code: _____

Mail to Harlequin Books: **In the U.S.:** P.O. Box 9069, Buffalo, NY 14269-9069; **In Canada:** P.O. Box 637, Fort Erie, Ontario, L4A 5X3

*No purchase necessary—for contest details send a self-addressed stamped envelope to: Silhouette's 20th Anniversary Contest, P.O. Box 9069, Buffalo, NY, 14269-9069 (include contest name on self-addressed envelope). Residents of Washington and Vermont may omit postage. Open to Cdn. (excluding Quebec) and U.S. residents who are 18 or over. Void where prohibited. Contest ends August 31, 2000.

PS20CON_R